Playlist

DOLLHOUSE- MELANIE MARTINEZ

CAROUSEL- MELANIE MARTINEZ

DAISY- ASHNIKKO

STUPID- ASHNIKKO

LET THE BODIES HIT THE FLOOR- DROWNING POOL

GRAVEYARD- HALSEY

ISAAC'S INSECTS- ISAAC DUNBAR

MIME- ISAAC DUNBAR

Warning

This book is extremely dark with triggering situations such as graphic gore and violence, arousal by murder, mentions of child abuse, psychological torture, suicide, and graphic sexual situations suited for 18+ readers.

Chapter 1

"One." *Stab*. A grunt punctuates my next word, "Two." *Stab*. Another grunt. "Freddy's coming for you," I sing, high-pitched and child-like. Blood spurts from his stab wounds, painting my face in a mosaic of red and gore.

The evil is seeping out of each hole I've made in his body. I can feel it, curling from the openings like smoke from the machines in nearly every corner of this house. I breathe in deep, *smelling* the evil coming out of him.

It smells like rotten egg and brimstone. It's how I know that I made the right judgement.

"Mortis, come hold his head," I order. My henchman listens immediately, gripping the man's head in his red hands, rendering him still as his black talons dig into the demon's face. His efforts to dislodge his head from Mortis's grip are so *cute*.

Gripping my pretty knife in my hand, I lean down closely and start working the pointed tip around the edge of the man's eyeball. It's my favorite knife. The handle is bright pink and swirls at the end. I've had this knife since I was a little girl, it's the only thing left I have of my mother's.

The wriggling parasite's screams intensify as my knife digs deeper, cutting around the inner edges of his eyelid as if I'm cutting a cake out of a pan. Blood spurts from the orifice, nearly splattering into my own eyes.

I dig the knife down and then push up, popping the eyeball from its socket.

His eyes are such a pretty blue.

"Three, four, better lock your door," I continue, my voice more subdued and distracted as pleasure sluices through every cell in my body and makes its way to the spot between my legs. Nothing gets me off more than my mission.

I throw the eyeball, the soft plop when it hits the wooden floor swallowed by the man's screams.

Silly little thing. No one will ever hear you scream.

I shoo Mortis away, no longer needing him at the moment. Mortis steps away, reclaiming his position in the corner of the room.

The man beneath me wriggles, calling me all kinds of choice names. His words are garbled through the blood pouring in *and* out of his mouth. Must've hit a lung.

Whoopsie.

In my distraction, he manages to dislodge me from his body. I fly sideways, landing awkwardly on my side, the knife coming within inches of my face. He stumbles to his feet, while my henchman, Mortis, takes a step towards him.

"Let him go," I order, watching my victim stagger to his feet and run out of the door. "I like the chase."

I stand, and calmly walk out of the room. The house is completely barricaded. Unbeknownst to the owners of the fair, my henchmen and I painted the windows shut so demons couldn't escape, while the emergency exit points are guarded by the rest of my henchmen.

There's no chance of his escape. And I love to play games.

"Five, six, grab a crucifix," I sing loudly, knowing he can hear me. I think *I'm* the one that needs the crucifix. The entire house is being filled with his rotten egg stench. I shudder, anxious to rid the house of it.

I look down either side of the hallway first. The smoke machines are off now, but the lack of ventilation in the house allows the colorful smoke to linger. They always dye the smoke all sorts of colors, creating a trippy effect when coupled with the strobe lights.

Now that the grounds outside of the house are empty, I turned all the flashing strobe lights back on and music filled with evil laughter, howling and zombie moans.

One of my henchmen, Jackal, stands at the very end of the hallway, the smoke concealing the majority of his body. What does poke through is his burnt face covered in boils, unnaturally wide smile stretching across his cheeks with blood dripping from his shark-like teeth and big yellow eyes. His makeup was always more grotesque than the others, which is why I make him guard the doors. His burnt skin looks and feels real to the touch, but it's all just makeup and prosthetics.

He doesn't move, instead continuing to stare at me.

He knows how much I enjoy the chase.

My eyes drop to the white hardwood floor, spotting a blood trail veering off to my left towards the staircase. He's trying to leave me.

I follow the blood trail, a smile on my face. "Seven, eight, gonna stay up late."

A thud from down the stairs resonates, right before a loud yelp. I giggle, already knowing he ran into one of my henchmen. Another loud bang and a frustrated scream. I hurry my steps, my heart pounding harder now that I know he's being a bad boy.

When I reach the bottom of the Barbie pink steps, I swing around the banister and sing, "Nine, ten, never sleep again."

"Fucking crazy ass bitch!" he screams from somewhere in the house.

I frown, hurt and angry by his words.

"I'm not crazy!" I screech. I take a deep, calming breath and arrange the smile back on my face. "I'm just passionate."

To my left and through pink double doors is the living room. More colorful smoke fills the room, but the open concept of the bottom floor thins it out, making it easier to see. On the bright robin's egg blue couch lays a mechanical pregnant woman giving birth to a demon. It feels like looking into the past, watching the birth of the current demon running rampant in my dollhouse.

The entire house is decorated in whites and pinks, with splashes of bright colors. The white stone fireplace in the corner of the living room is lined with dolls, all their faces melted or dirty, with patches of hair ripped from their skulls. The sight always makes me happy.

Excited once more, I head down the hallway leading back to the kitchen. His blood trail leads back there. Based off the handprint smudges and streaks of blood, he must've fell in there. Probably when he ran into Cronus.

After all, Cronus is the size of a Mac truck. He must be a body builder in his free time. His neck is the size of a tree trunk, his arms even bigger. Bulging veins cover the entirety of his body, especially his cock. It looks as if he has no mouth and eyes at all, convincing prosthetics covering them, so it looks as if his face is blank. I never bothered to ask how he sees—he's a mute. I figured the eye prosthetics are see-through, as he never seems to have any problems seeing.

I walk through the kitchen and see the demon with an axe in his hands, struggling to raise the heavy axe. He's losing blood quickly, the adrenaline the only thing keeping his body functioning.

Pulsing rage has my eyes widening and lighting my insides on fire when he manages to swing the axe into the wall.

How dare he!

He can't get through my henchmen, so he's going to desecrate my pretty dollhouse and try to breakout through the walls.

"You're really hurting my feelings, demon," I say, announcing my arrival. He freezes at my voice. He's as pale as a ghost, the color bleached from his skin. When he turns to see me and the angry scowl on my face, he turns and attempts to swing the axe more vigorously. Desperately. But he only manages to lodge the blade into the wall once more.

He's too weak now.

"Cronus!" I screech, stomping my foot. "He's making my dollhouse ugly!"

Cronus comes walking in the room, but the demon doesn't acknowledge him. He's too focused on his escape.

I point my finger. "Get him to stop," I whine.

Cronus walks over to the man. Feeling my henchman coming for him, the guy swings his axe around wildly, a crazed gleam in his one eye. He releases a battle cry, but Cronus easily swipes the sharp weapon from the man's grip. He grabs either end of the axe and cracks it over his knee, snapping it in two like a twig.

The man's eye widens. It used to be a pretty blue, but his pupil has completely taken over, morphing it into a nearly black eye—just like a true demon. His eye darts around the room, sliding past me as if I'm not there to find an escape route, but there is none.

You can't hide from fate. That's the funny thing about destiny, even if you try to escape it, it will always find you.

Cronus's arm snaps out faster than a whip and grabs the man by his throat. He brings him close to his face. The man thrashes in his hold, and screams in his face, a mix of fear and frustration. I join Cronus's side, but he doesn't even pay me attention. Not when there's a behemoth of a man holding you into his missing face.

"Bring him back to my room," I order, turning around without another glance. Cronus drags him behind me, ignoring the punches and kicks to his limbs. I enter my cute, pink bedroom, Mortis still waiting in the corner of the room. He leans against the wall, arms crossed over his chest with a bored look on his face. He almost looks frozen.

I don't pay him any mind yet, my attention too focused on the demon being carted in the room behind me. Adrenaline surges, and my hands nearly tremble with the desire beginning to course through my system.

Cronus throws the demon on the floor and exits the room, trusting me to finish my life's work. Even with several stab wounds and a missing eye, the demon still has fight in him. It's disgusting.

I climb back on top of his body, resuming my original position. He wriggles under me, trying his best to buck me off of him. The feel of his body squirming beneath me repulses me, but the blood coating his body makes me shiver. I love the sight, but it's not enough.

I bring my knife down with all my strength, plunging it deep into his torso. I lift up and stab a few more times. He's screaming again, his eye widening from the pain. I revel in the sound, it's like music to my ears.

He lifts up out of instinct, still screaming. Using the distraction to my advantage, I bring the knife directly down on top of his head. His body goes slack, and his nerves misfire. His body convulses as his eye rolls to the back of his head.

I rip the knife from his head and start stabbing frantically, the feeling of my pretty knife cutting through flesh and bone is making my clit pulse. I sing Freddy's song aloud again, each word punctuated by another stab. The smell of rotten egg intensifies, filling my nose and becoming stronger until it fills the room as densely as the smoke in the hallway.

At some point my eyes roll and my tired arm slackens as pure bliss shudders through my body. I grind my body against the empty vessel, high off the kill. Euphoria wracks through my spine and within seconds, I'm coming hard. I continue to grind my hips against the man, drawing out my orgasm and wringing every last drop from my pussy. I'm flooding him, my juices mixing with his blood.

I come down, shuddering and groaning as I do.

When I go to lift my knife again, a soft voice interrupts me.

"I think he's dead," Mortis comments dryly from behind me. I smile at his tone and glance over my shoulder, noting he's adorned in his costume. I smile wider. He's *always* in costume. All of my henchmen are. Always playing their part because this is what we do. This is how we eradicate evil from the world, one town at a time.

Mortis's face is painted blood red, dark black circles around his eyes, spikes glued down the middle of his bald head, and red contacts in his eyes. He wears gloves with talons for fingers. And they're really fucking sharp. I've watched those sharp little blades sink into flesh and cut bone. I've licked the blood clean from them, cutting my tongue in the process and reveling in the euphoria of doing this world real justice.

A *real* service.

Daddy always said he was the one doing this world a service, but he was wrong.

He was the one corrupting this world, while I do my best to save it.

"These people would be lost without me, Sibel. God chose me to carry out His law and I will not let Him down."

Shaking the memory loose, I look back down at the sack of wasted flesh between my thighs. The second he came into my house, he *reeked* of evil. I could smell it on him from a mile away. His girlfriend, clinging to him like she'd slip off the edge of Earth otherwise, smelled like freshly bloomed roses. The girl didn't know the vileness she was clinging to.

I saved her.

The man below me is hardly a man now. My knife has disappeared into his face so many times that all that's left is brain matter, meat and bone. His teeth poke out from the gore. I cock my head. He has several cavities—another testament to the malevolence residing inside him. When you carry a demon in your soul, it rots you from the inside out. Black, rotting teeth is a big indicator.

I smile again. I chose well.

I stand up, my white gown dripping red onto the hardwood floor. Timothy will come in soon and clean it up for me, while Mortis properly disposes of the body. My henchmen treat me well. In return, I reward them fondly.

Waving a hand at the man, signaling Mortis to take him, my loyal henchman walks forward, lifts the dead man up from under his arms and drags him out. The guests are long gone now, the operators and food truck employees have abandoned their posts and left for the night. All staff are required to leave the grounds when the fair closes—my henchmen included, but they find ways to sneak back in once the grounds are empty.

It's safe for Mortis now. I'm not entirely sure where he puts the bodies, as our scenery is ever-changing. He always manages to figure it out, though, and I trust him to do his job well.

We've been doing this for five years and haven't gotten caught, thanks to Mortis and Timothy.

Timothy comes clambering in. With the house shut down for the night, we're all able to walk freely. All day, they're confined to their stations, going through the same old jump scares with every guest that walks through my dollhouse while I haunt from inside of the walls. My poor babies get so bored. That's why I always give them a taste when I cast my judgement.

With Satan's Affair travelling around the country during the fall months, we've become quite famous. A travelling Halloween fair, with dozens of haunted houses, small thrill rides and plenty of food to gorge yourself on. Every year, the theme of our houses change to avoid our guests walking through the same houses year after year, being scared by the same monsters.

This year, my house is called *Annie's Playhouse*. The entire house is decorated to look like a child's dollhouse. I quite like the décor this year. Pink and frills everywhere, boas and little dolls to play with when I get bored. I play dress-up with the costumes, dancing in front of the mirror and singing my favorite song, *Ring Around the Rosey*. Sometimes, when I'm *really* bored, I'll cut the skin from whatever demon I've cast judgement on and use their skin as a dress.

My henchmen love watching me play. When I'm happy, they're happy.

Several people work in my house during operation, but only five of them are loyal to me. I assigned each of my henchmen with a specific job. They come around when their presence is needed. Mortis and Timothy are my favorite—which is why I let them dispose of the sickness after I've finished. The other three are appointed with luring the demon away after I've cast my judgment.

"Would you like me to clean you up, Sibby?" Timothy asks from below me, his muscular back on display. Timothy has the best body out of the bunch, so he doesn't wear a shirt during operation. Bloody handprints decorate his chest and stomach, along with plastic moldings of deep gouges from fingernails. They look so real.

He's kneeling before me now, cleaning up the pool of blood that's gathered beneath my feet. I slip off my ruined slippers and tiptoe over the blood, pretending its lava that will burn if it touches me.

Timothy watches me prance, a smile on his clown face. Royal blue tufts of hair sprout from the side of his otherwise bald head, a stark contrast to his white face, red lips and the red triangles decorating either side of his baby blue eyes. He's got razor sharp teeth behind his plump lips, but he's always careful not to cut me when he licks my pussy.

"Yes, please, Timothy," I respond, making my way over to the rocking chair in the corner of the room. During the day, a mannequin of a woman sits here, rocking her decapitated baby while singing a haunting lullaby.

Timothy finishes the floor first, mopping up the blood, stuffing the rags in a black garbage bag and setting the trash in the corner to take out later. Next, he brings over fresh washcloths and starts wiping the blood off my face and neck.

His touch is gentle and loving. I love when Timothy cleans me, because he stares at me as if I'm his favorite prop. When the blood is clean from my face, he works his way down to my arms and hands. Then, to my legs.

My breath hitches. This is always my favorite part.

Gently, he rubs the cloth on my feet, and works his way up my leg, massaging my calves as he does. I groan, shivers racing up my spine from the mix of pain and pleasure. My pussy heats, juices gathering between my thighs as his hands slowly work their way towards my center.

He lifts my gown, baring my waist completely. I don't wear panties under my gown. I find them very restricting for my henchmen.

Naturally, I spread my legs wide on the rocking chair so Timothy has full access. He spares me one last glance, making sure he has my permission before darting his tongue out and gliding the wet muscle up my slit.

A gasp leaves my throat as pleasure engulfs me. My little gasp is all the encouragement he needs. He settles in deeper, covering the entirety of my pussy with his mouth and gorging himself on me. His tongue thrusts inside me, little sharp stabs that wring out pure euphoria. When he stiffens his tongue and licks at my clit, I nearly lose it.

My eyes roll and my hips grind against his face. My hand grabs the back of his head, bringing him closer and nearly suffocating the clown on my juices.

Mortis comes back in the room just as my orgasm crests. The oxygen depletes from my lungs as fireworks explode in the back of my eyes. Ecstasy wracks my body, and I can't control the shuddering that overcomes me as I ride out the waves against Timothy's face.

Only when the orgasm begins to drift, do I sag against the rocking chair, my body utterly spent. Timothy pulls away, smacking his red-painted lips like he just had the best meal of his life. I smile in appreciation.

He's so cute.

Glancing up, Mortis already has his pants around his ankles and his cock gripped firmly in his fist. I lick my lips, salivating at the sight before me. Mortis doesn't bother painting the rest of his body red, just his face. My henchman is a very tall man, though extremely skinny. He has no meat to his body, but I don't mind—not when he carries all the meat between his legs.

Timothy moves aside, letting Mortis step forward, pick me up and sink in the chair beneath me. He settles me on his lap, his hard ridge cocooned perfectly in my pussy. Timothy prepared me plenty, leaving me dripping wet. I grind my hips, sliding my center up and down his shaft and pulling deep moans from both of us.

Having enough of the torture, he lifts me just enough to pose the crown of his head at my entrance, and then slams me down, lifting his bony hips in tandem.

My head falls back, a long moan releasing from my throat, much like a wolf would howl at the moon. I let Mortis do all the work, basking in his attention and need to take control. Loving the way he owns my body as he pounds into me. The sound of skin slapping, and grunts fill the room as Timothy leaves to dispose of the trash.

I tip my head back, a long moan releasing from my throat. The coil in my stomach tightens. It feels like a rope fraying at the seams, a heavy weight pulling it apart until it just... *snaps.*

I let loose a scream as another orgasm crashes through me. Mortis grunts from below me, pistoning his hips faster, sloppier, chasing his own orgasm. Soon, he finds what he's searching for, stilling beneath me and letting out a long groan as his cum fills me up.

A wide smile breaks across my pale face.

I don't do the jump scares like my henchmen, but I still dress the part in the case

I'm seen. I make my face up to look like a dolly with a broken face, cracks and fissures running through my skin. Only at night, do I wipe the makeup clean.

Without it, I'm just a plain jane. Brown hair, brown eyes and an unremarkable face. I'm not ugly, but I won't be featured on any magazines in my lifetime.

That's okay. I don't need to be beautiful when I'm doing exactly what I was created to do.

Not a single soul passes through the threshold of this house without me casting judgment—determining if evil resides in their soul. As they make their way through the maze of my dollhouse, I watch from inside the walls.

They're *all* judged. Every single one of them.

If one fails, I sing my songs and my henchmen will lead them away—separate them from family or friends. And when they're well and truly alone, I strike.

They're never to be seen again, and I've cleansed this world of one less demon.

Chapter 2

"Mortis, shush!" I reprimand, slapping away his hand. His hand retreats, but I know it's going to come creeping back up my thigh in just a moment.

Mortis is the neediest out of the bunch, though you wouldn't know it unless he wanted you to. It's because he has severe Mommy issues. She was a crack addict when pregnant with him, and when he was born, she ignored his existence almost completely. Up until she overdosed, and he got put in the system at a young age.

The other four have similar childhoods. All with fucked up parents that abused them in one way or another. Baine was abused sexually—his father had a penchant for oral sex. He's never said it, but I think that's why he starves himself. He has a weird relationship with putting anything in his mouth, even if it's food. He's the only one out of the bunch that won't go down on me, and I've never pushed him to.

Considering Cronus is mute, I've never heard his story from him. I know he's capable of speaking—he just refuses to. I looked into him once before and saw that his mother locked him in a closet when he was young and refused to let him out for months. He went silent after screaming for his mother until he lost his voice and hasn't spoken since.

Jackal and Timothy grew up in the foster care system since as long as they could remember. Moving from house to house—one abuser to the next. They've told me stories about their experiences in some of the foster homes, and they nearly brought me to tears.

We've all been deprived of love and find plenty of it in each other.

My dollhouse has been settled into its new resting spot in Houston, Texas, and the fair will open soon. Mortis has been feeling me up all fucking day, trying to fuck me when I'm trying to focus. I have the feeling he's going to call the rest of my henchmen in soon to try and relax me. They know when they gang up on me, all their cocks surrounding me—I can't resist.

I don't need that distraction right now. What I *need* is to focus.

There's been times I've come to a city and haven't been able to sense evil at all in the guests who arrive. I know they're out there, but something kept them away from me. Kept them from walking into their deserved fate.

Those days are the worst. It's a day wasted, no walking evil to be rid of. Still tainting this Earth with their rot. I always plead to our creator, *why* did you let them get away? Why let scum continue to live and breathe another day?

It feels like parasites are crawling beneath my skin when those days come to pass. Which is why I've made it my mission to make sure the evil comes to me. I can't risk letting the demons slip away. If I do, they'll continue to taint this world with their filth.

I think back to the latest demon I killed, how his girlfriend was hanging on him when they walked through my house. Her roses would've wilted and crumbled from the tar he surely would've spread on her petals.

Just like Mommy's did when Daddy tainted her with his sins.

I need to prevent that. This world deserves to be pure. Mommy deserved to stay pure, too. And even though she'll never get to experience it, her flowers wilted so I could be born into this world and create a *new* world—one without evil.

During the day, the houses are shut down and the dressed-up monsters walk the fairgrounds. They scare the little kids, chase after the adults and send them running towards whatever money-sucking machine they reach first. Whether it's an ATM or a credit card terminal that grants them access to greasy food and endless tickets.

I like to explore during the day, sniffing out the immoral ones in the crowd. On a good day, I get overwhelmed by the amount of black souls walking this Earth. I can't kill them all, but I try my best to lure them towards my dollhouse.

Usually I just approach them, doing my job and scaring them. They laugh and smile, while I shudder from my need to execute them. I adorn an innocent face and tell them to come play with me in my dollhouse. I make promises of how fun it'll be, a wicked smile on my face. *That*, I don't have to fake.

Most times, it works like a charm.

Then when night falls, I eagerly wait within the walls. *Annie's Playhouse* only allows up to ten people to come through at a time, that way my house doesn't become overcrowded. It grants me all the time I need to watch each guest closely, following them for a bit while I decide if their souls are tainted or not before moving onto the next.

I don't know all the sins that dirty a soul. The obvious rape or murdering someone for nothing else than one's own gain or pleasure will taint a soul. But I don't believe all of the demons have committed such heinous crimes. Some are smarter, keeping their darkness deep within. Some might peruse the dark web, jacking off to child porn or reading cookbooks on how to grill human meat. Some of them take their pleasures in other species, fucking animals and recording it. The ones that don't fuck them usually kill them. Innocent animals succumbed to torture because there's a sickness residing in humans.

Or maybe they don't do any of those things, but just simply desire to. After all, every crime begins with an innocent thought—a simple desire that's nothing more than a kink or a *what if.* Until those desires evolve and become actions.

There are surely a million different reasons, and I don't care to figure them all out. They all smell the same. Rotten and evil. Just like the pure tend to have sweet or nature scents. The flowers are my favorite—they're the purest.

I've noticed the decrepit souls as far back as I can remember. Mommy and Daddy were members of the Saintly Baptist Church. Daddy loved to bring in people to worship his word, citing that he's God's disciple and his word carries power.

People believed him. *Thousands* of people believed him. *He* became their God. At night, when Mommy would go to sleep, I'd wake up to the sounds of screams. I'd sneak out of the room, tiptoe down the hall and see several naked people in the room with Daddy, pleasuring him. From what I saw, he never returned the favors—at least not really. He'd let men and women pleasure him with their mouths and then ride him while he just took the pleasure like a greedy fucking sloth.

When I had asked him why he lets all of these people do those things to him, he had said that the fluids in his body were God's nectar, and the only way to truly bless people with God is by them draining the fluids from him, in whatever form they chose.

I wasn't so sure that was true, but I didn't argue. I knew even then it was pointless. Daddy smelled like rotten eggs. So did a lot of the people in our Church, draining him of his nectar. But I didn't understand that I was shown these things for a purpose—to eradicate these demons. At the time, I was too worried about Mommy and her increasingly depleting body. She turned into nothing but skin and bones, an empty shell of a woman who had little left in her but her aching soul.

Mommy smelled like black roses. Daddy tainted her, and her petals started to wilt and decay.

I lost her when I didn't have to. If she would've removed us from that evil Church with an even worse dictator, we could've had a happy life. I suppose her death wasn't all in vain—it gave me my purpose in life. If I can just extinguish all the evil, then I can finally live in a pure world with my flower garden of people.

Huffing, I stand up and glare down at Mortis. He's been needy today. I don't *like* needy.

"What is wrong with you today?" I hiss, putting my hands on my hips.

"You're on edge," he says, his voice monotone. Mortis never speaks with much inflection in his voice. "I want to calm you down."

I sneer. "The only thing that's going to calm me down is catching another demon. You should know that by now."

He just stares at me, his face blank and lifeless.

Growling, I whip around and storm out of the house. No one has arrived yet for the haunted houses, which I'm thankful for. I don't like interacting with the others. They're terrible actors, dirty up my house, and then leave their messes for me to clean up later.

During the Halloween season, I live in the house. I don't like to leave, should an opportunity arise for a cleansing and I need to act quickly. My henchmen will leave with the rest of the crew at the end of the day, and then sneak back in after the fair closes.

Once I've cast my judgement and my henchmen separate the demon from whoever they came with, I'll pressure point them until they're unconscious, tie them up, and keep duct tape over their mouths. Whatever screams and noise they make once they wake up blends in with the screams of terror from the guests. I make sure they're unconscious when the staff are shutting down the place, but once everyone is gone, they are moved back into my playroom.

Normal people—the ones who occupy this world without contributing much to it—they wouldn't understand. Whether they're pure or not, murder is wrong in their eyes, even if it's justified. It doesn't matter that I do this for *them*.

They're just weak.

Stepping out of my house, I inhale deeply. Greasy food, mud, and fabricated scents waft towards me, filling my senses first. It takes me a minute to adjust to the distracting odors and differentiate the smell of people's souls apart from their perfumes and the surrounding aromas.

I wander the fairgrounds; the crunch of brittle grass blades a soothing sound beneath my thin white slippers. My feet itch from the little pinpricks from the grass, but I don't mind. I steal a pack of cotton candy when the vendor isn't looking and trounce off with my treat. I happily pluck sweet, sugary fluffs from the cone and plop them in my mouth as I observe the guests.

Already I'm picking up on the stench. With so many people packing the grounds, it takes me awhile to pinpoint the exact source. Moving towards the stench, I continue to observe while I continuously inhale, much like a K9 with paraphernalia.

The smell is definitely rotten. I wriggle my nose, stopping mid-step to sniff out the direction. Someone knocks into my shoulder, jolting me forward and knocking my cotton candy out of my hand. I watch the cloud of sugar roll across the filthy ground, picking up mud and grass.

I frown, deep sadness swirling in the pit of my stomach.

The girl turns, her eyes wide. "I'm so sorry," she rushes out. She's got pretty white-blonde hair and brown eyes with beautiful porcelain skin.

She'd be real fun to cut up.

I glare at her and step into her space. She freezes, flinching away from me when I put my nose to her neck and inhale deeply.

"Dude, what the fuck?" she bursts, snapping out of her stupor and stumbling away. "Did you just fucking *smell* me?" she asks incredulously, staring at me like I'm a creep. My dark brown hair is piled into high pigtails, sloppy red lips and my face painted to look like a doll's glass face is cracking must look creepy.

My eyes nearly roll when I pick up her sweet aroma. She smells like daisies.

"You smell good," I answer, smiling so she's not mad at me anymore. *I'm* not mad at *her* anymore, and she's the one that ruined my cotton candy.

Her friend, who was standing behind her, walks up beside my little daisy. She's also staring at me like I'm a freak.

I don't like that. I just was trying to make sure she wasn't rotten.

"Do you not understand personal space?" her friend snaps. Her orange hair is frizzing, and too many freckles cover her face. I sniff her, too. She smells like poppies. I like her smell, and if I didn't want to preserve the good people in this world, I'd try to bottle her smell. Maybe soaking her flesh for a little while to see if that'll collect the scent.

"You're at a haunted fair. Get used to the creepiness," I retort. When they just stare at me, seemingly at a loss for words, I give them a wide toothy smile and continue walking. They'll probably stay away from the dollhouse now, but that's okay. My dollhouse is meant to trap the bad people in the world.

I prance off, getting sucked into the crowd. I feel their lingering, nasty glares and it hurts my feelings. I freeze again, mid-step, remembering my cotton candy is stuck in the mud. Tears spring to my eyes and I frown deeply. I really liked that cotton candy. It was a pretty pink color, just like my pretty pink knife and pretty pink dollhouse.

I'm not happy. I'm not happy at all.

Stomping through the crowd, I no longer care to be polite. The daisy and poppy girls ruined my whole day. They really, really hurt my feelings. Anger begins to curdle in my stomach, replacing the hurt with rage.

"This is why you don't have friends, Sibel. You're a freak and everyone can see it. God has seen the illness in your brain and made sure everyone else can see it, too."

Fuck what God thinks. I had said it then, too, and Daddy forced my hand on a hot stove for it. The scar from that isn't physical, but I feel it in my *sick* brain.

The potent fury rises, building in my chest and climbing to my throat. My hand trembles with the need to curl a knife in my fist and plunge it deep into someone's throat. I long to hear the gurgling as they choke on their blood. Their dull eyes, wide with fear. I can almost see their lives flashing in their dilated irises.

I ache for it.

Curling my fist tight to abate the shaking, I focus on the smell.

My fiery eyes search the crowd, the rotten odor growing stronger as I plunge through people. One girl pushes me after I shove past her. I stumble, righting myself just before my face plants into the ground.

I'm so angry, and it's starting to make people notice me. I don't want Management to catch wind of the angry doll pushing people around. It's just... I just wanted this to be a good day!

Huffing and storming off before I do something silly like kill someone in cold blood, I rush back towards my dollhouse. My anger is overwhelming me, and I can no longer concentrate.

Killing someone without a good reason would be a sin. Most people don't have the guts to do what I do, serve this world the way I do. But to kill an innocent person? I don't even want to consider it.

I storm back into the house. Dusk is approaching, which means staff will start trickling in my dollhouse, preparing for when the doors open. I need to hide. I turn towards the small door hidden in the corner of the room, hidden behind a life-sized doll. With the house being cast in darkness and flickering lights, no one has noticed it thus far. I make sure to cut out the doors in the walls in precise locations, as to not draw the eye.

Quickly climbing in, I shut the door gently behind me. It's eerie inside the walls, but I've grown accustomed to them. Haunted houses aren't built like normal housing. They're not meant to sustain life, and long ago, I discovered that they create large gaps in between the walls when building them. They do this on purpose so they can hide the wiring and mechanisms but make it accessible if something breaks. In all my time here, I've only had one electrician come in my space to fix a power outage in one of the rooms.

When I pick a new haunted house, I puncture holes in the walls to access my own tunnel system, and then carefully place peepholes in every room and hallway for when it's time to cast my judgement. In the end, this is where I end up spending the majority of my time during operating hours.

I don't mind the seclusion. It gives me time to myself, to relax and focus on all the ways I'm going to fuck my henchmen in the demon's blood that dare enter my house.

I slide my pretty knife out of my white nightgown, just to bring me some type of peace in the midst of the raging storm in my head. My dresses are gaudy and frilly, but I love dressing up in them. Plenty of doll costumes are provided to the staff, all I need to do is take what I want and leave the rest for them to pick through.

Wooden beams cut through my pathway. There are dim LED strips that line the bottom of the walls, lighting the path for any electricians who need to walk through here. It provides the perfect amount of lighting without being bright enough to cast any of my shadows through the cracks in the walls.

In every nook and cranny in the tunnels, spiders spin their webs. I wouldn't dare swipe them down. I love spiders. I love what they stand for. Predators—no matter who or what you are. They're viewed as dangerous and something to be feared.

I'd want to be a spider. I'd love for my house to symbolize them one year so I can dress up as a spider queen and sink my teeth into a sinner's throat. My anger abates as I fantasize, and the juncture between my thighs grows slick.

I quietly make way through the hallways, climbing up the stairs they put inside the walls. The haunted house will be opening within the hour. Already I can hear other employees showing up, most already adorned in their full costumes, giggling about all the things they're going to do to scare people.

In the walls, I hear all kinds of conversations I'm not supposed to be privy to. Most of the time, I don't bother listening. I'm not concerned with other's trivial drama and concerns. Who fucked whose boyfriend. But one of the girl's conversations catches my attention as I'm passing one of the bedrooms.

I pause, and creep closer towards the wall.

"He's coming to visit me tonight, but I really don't know if I want him to," the girl says. It takes a moment to register that she's crying. Seeking out the small hole to peer into the room, I put my eye to the hole and look around.

The girls are in the bathroom, ignoring the mannequin in the shower that's being electrocuted by the running water. They haven't turned on the noise effect yet, otherwise the mannequin would be screaming its head off and overpowering their conversation.

The girl crying is Jennifer. A tall blonde that has always been super sweet. She's dressed in her costume. White painted body, with black rimmed eyes and a shredded dress. She looks demonic, but she smells like roses.

Jennifer is speaking to another coworker of ours, Sarah. Sarah smells like grass to me. Not appealing, but not evil either. She's one of the drama starters in my house. She's always tossing her mousey brown hair over her shoulder and rolling her eyes at people.

And I guarantee the minute Jennifer is done complaining to her, she's going to run off and repeat every single word she heard.

She's a bitch, but not evil.

"Why?" Sarah asks, resting a pale hand on Jennifer's shoulder. Sarah's also dressed up like a little doll, though her face is painted to look pretty. She's supposed to fool guests into thinking she's harmless until she opens her mouth and reveals razor-sharp teeth.

Her costume is a metaphor for her personality, I've noticed.

"Last night," Jennifer starts, looking a tad nervous. "I got really drunk. And I don't remember much, but I think Gary had sex with me when I asked him not to."

Sarah gasps, her eyes widening and hand flying over her mouth in shock. I curl my lip, disgusted with what I just heard.

"He, like, raped you?" Sarah breathes behind her hand.

Another tear tracks down Jennifer's face. She bites her bottom lip and nods her head.

"Yeah," she chokes out. "I think so. I only remember bits and pieces, but he definitely had sex with me and I..." she trails over, a sob wracking her throat and cutting off her sentence. I step closer, molding myself to the wall as if that's going to offer her any comfort.

Sarah places a comforting hand on Jennifer's arm. "It's okay, Jenny, you can tell me," she assures.

Jennifer sniffles, wiping snot from her nose. Her costume paint comes off with it. "I r-remember telling him to stop. Like, several times. I think I tried even pushing him away because I didn't feel good. I remember him pinning my arms down and telling me to shut up when I kept asking him to stop. And he wouldn't!" she ends her sentence on a wail, dropping her face into her hands. Sarah wraps herself around Jennifer, holding her close as Jennifer continues to sob into her hands.

I take a step back, my breath short as black thoughts swirl in my head. Jennifer was raped by her boyfriend. Only someone evil could do something like that.

My thoughts spiral into a deep abyss. She said he was coming here tonight. Her rapist boyfriend will be in my house. And I...

I will cleanse this world again tonight. And set Jennifer free.

Chapter 3

about eighteen
years old

"*Did you just say no to me?*"

Daddy holds his fork halfway to his mouth, bloody red juices dripping off his steak and splashing onto the plate. I stare at the droplets instead of meeting his eyes.

"*Look at me!*" *he bellows, slamming his other fist down onto the table. Everyone gasps, jumping away as water glasses topple over and spill onto laps and cutlery falls to the floor. It takes a powerful man to make a table of this size tremble. A table that fits all his children—all eighteen of them and counting.*

Curling my lip, I bring my eyes to his.

Daddy likes to embarrass me in front of my siblings, but he hasn't realized that I don't get embarrassed in front of them. They all look at him with the same disdain—they're all just sheep. Too scared and brainwashed to speak out against him.

I'm sure some of them truly believe God speaks to Daddy. I just see a wolf in grandma's clothing.

Mommy used to read me Red Riding Hood at night, and when I had asked if Daddy was the big bad wolf in her story, she ran out of the room in tears. The next day, she burned the book and said that book was made by the Devil and she should've never read it to me.

"Did you. Say. No. To. Me?" he asks, enunciating each word through bared teeth. There's meat stuck in his teeth, and the sight makes my stomach curl with revulsion. I want to see his meat stuck in another animal's teeth. What I would give to see a lion rip his body to pieces and feast on his black heart.

"Is that what you heard me say?" I challenge quietly.

Daddy said that I'm to gather all of the girls tonight and bring them to him for his nightly ritual. Where he feeds them God's nectar. I said no and called him unholy.

His face grows red, and his nearly black eyes bulge from his head. He's an ugly man. Thinning brown hair that shows his scalp in several areas. A squared jaw and a hooked nose. He's Romanian, and still speaks with an accent. He uses his accent like a weapon, along with his charm and charisma. That's how he gets all of his followers. That's how he brainwashes them.

"Put your hand on the table."

"No," I whisper.

He laughs. It's an evil laugh that shows me his patience is wearing thin.

"If you don't, I will punish your mother. She's not doing a particularly good job of raising you."

My mask cracks for just a moment. My lip trembles from the threat, and I have to bite it sharply to stop the tremors. He caught it, though. Daddy knows she's my weakness. He knows how much I love her.

Slowly, I rest my hand on the table, keeping it far away from him.

"Bring it here."

I grit my teeth as tears burn my eyes. I won't let them escape—that would only spur him on.

"Did the Lord say that I need to be punished?" I ask, stalling.

"Yes, he did, Sibel. He sees everything you do. All the naughty things you do when you don't think I can see you. And how you continue to disrespect God's only disciple. How do you think that makes Him feel?"

I don't answer. If I tell Daddy that I don't believe God speaks to him, he will kill me. That is the foundation the Saintly Baptist Church is made on. God speaks to Daddy, and he relays His message to his faithful believers. They worship Daddy, they don't worship God.

For whatever reason, they believe his lies. Even though I've only ever seen Daddy do evil things. Unholy things.

"Bring your hand here, Sibel," he orders again when I don't answer.

I take a deep breath and slam my hand on the table in front of him, defiance set in my jawline. He stares at me, not making a move for a solid thirty seconds. And then as quick as a whip, he raises his fork and stabs into the top of my hand.

A yelp escapes, and I squeeze my eyes shut against the pain.

"Jesus had his hands nailed to the cross. I'm only showing you a morsel of the pain he felt when he died on the cross, for people like you. For your sins. You spit in his face every time you disobey me and the word of God. Remember that, Sibel."

He retracts the fork, and blood spurts from the four tiny wounds in my hand. If he didn't completely fuck up my hand for life, it will leave a barely noticeable scar. Funny how something so painful will heal and disappear like it didn't nearly bring me to my knees.

That's what God wants, doesn't He? Me on my knees, praying for strength and perseverance.

I shake like a leaf, trying to hold in my tears. I want to run to my room and cry. Curl up in a ball and try to breathe through the pain.

But Daddy would never let me run and hide. He'd rather I be forced to show weakness in front of my siblings. He'd rather I embarrass myself.

My wet glare meets all the dim eyes staring at me. None of them make a move to help me. Defend me. Soothe me. They just stare on like lifeless zombies, desensitized to the punishments Daddy's constantly doling out to me. They're used to my defiance. And they're used to leaving me to stand alone.

I meet Daddy's glare, his lip curling. I didn't give a big enough reaction. I'm not hurting enough for his satisfaction. And that makes the bleeding wounds in my hand feel a little bit less painful, and a little bit more like consummation.

So, I take another deep breath, pick up my spoon with my left hand and scoop a mouthful of mashed potatoes in my mouth.

He stares at me, his face smoothing into impassivity. But I see the glimmer in his eye. The evil thoughts he's having of murdering me in cold blood.

He's not God's disciple. He's Lucifer's little bitch.

"Where are you, Mommy?" I ask, my voice floating around an empty room.

She's been missing since yesterday, soon after dinner. Daddy called a meeting for all of his mistresses, and she hasn't come back yet.

The anxiety started when I saw some of the other women make their way back to their rooms, dried tear streaks on their cheeks. When Mommy didn't return with them, fear bloomed in the pit of my stomach and has only grown larger as the hours pass by.

I'm curled up in a ball, my stomach aching from the concern for Mommy. This is all my fault.

If I had just listened to Daddy, Mommy wouldn't be wherever she is. Probably in pain. Alone. Scared for her life. I nearly choke on the next thought. Dead.

What if he killed her?

Would Daddy really do something like that—murder an innocent woman in cold blood?

Yes. That little voice in my head whispers, deepening my ever-growing terror.

I didn't want to lead those young girls to what would certainly traumatize them. They're new to the Church. Their parents joined, and were all too happy to pleasure Daddy. Do things to him that I've never read about in the Bible.

I didn't want to see those girls, not much younger than me, end up as mothers. Just like Mommy did with me and my siblings. I was Mommy's first born. She had let it slip before that she was only eleven years old.

At the time, I didn't understand the gravity of that information. The second it left her mouth, her eyes widened, and her face paled to a sickly gray color. She snapped at me to never repeat that to anyone outside of the Church— not that I'm even allowed to leave the Church. She pinched my hand until I promised her, pure terror shining in her eyes.

Mommy gave birth to two more children before her body gave out and she was no longer able to bear children. Daddy said she has completed God's mission, and now her life's purpose is to help raise the children.

Daddy hasn't been happy with how I've been raised for several years. Probably because I'm unhappy. The more I see, the more I want to run from this rotten place, where decay is soaked into the walls.

Flowers can't survive in a place like this. I've already seen so many wilt beneath Daddy's iron fist.

A sob wracks my throat. I slap a hand over my mouth to keep the sound in. No one can hear me cry. I keep my hand glued to my face as I rock back and forth, pinching my eyes shut as I try to keep the black thoughts from growing.

The tears leak through anyways, but I don't make another sound.

She's okay. She's okay. She has to be okay.

"*Come back to me, Mommy,*" *I whisper into the pool of tears in my hand.*

"*I can't do this without you.*"

Chapter 4

Plumes of colorful smoke waft through the foyer as screams of terror ring out, filling the room with shades of greens, purples and reds. Strobe lights flicker, inducing a terrifying effect as monsters chase after guests. They look like creatures flickering in and out of portals from Hell, their bodies being pulled back and forth between the human realm and their true home. Giggles, screams and stomping footsteps follow soon after.

They run from monsters as if they have anywhere to hide.

I linger behind the walls on the bottom floor where a group of four enters the house. I watch them closely through the peepholes, inhaling their essence.

A garden of flowers. Sweet, innocent, pure.

I smile, watching them scream their heads off and push into each other, trying to escape from the monsters chasing after them. One doll carries a kitchen knife in her hand, fake blood dripping off the sharpened point as she slowly stalks after the girls.

They'll run from the doll, but they won't be able to escape her.

I let the group of girls move on, staying in my spot and await the next group. The first group of five that came before the four girls are on their way out. While not every single person from the first group smelled like fresh flowers, they didn't reek of evil, either.

The second the first group leaves, the door opens, and six people stumble in. Two men and four girls. The girls are already hunched together, hanging on each other's arms with their hands linked so tightly, their knuckles are bleached white. Nervous giggles emanating from their pretty mouths. The two guys behind them are attempting to act macho, though I can see the whites of their shifty eyes from here.

Satan's Affair is a world-renowned fair for a reason. We are known to have the scariest haunted houses in the country—short of the few places that allow their employees to lay hands on the guests, even going as far as torturing them.

Those haunted houses are classless. We don't need to touch our guests in order to scare them half to death.

The hours pass by slowly. Groups of people coming in and out, their throats turning hoarse from screams. At one point, a girl peed her pants and had to walk out with a huge wet spot in her jeans. I wanted to rip a couple people's throats out from laughing at the poor, embarrassed girl.

But I refrained because none of them were evil—just callous.

Of all the people that passed through my dollhouse, none of them have the telltale rot emanating from them. Frustration grows, and I'm beginning to feel restless.

I want to feel blood soaking into my flesh, feel my knife cutting through sinew and muscle and tearing apart delicate skin. But I can't just kill anyone. I refuse to kill innocents. I'm not an evil person.

I pace behind the walls, restlessness making my skin crawl. Mortis leaves his post at one point, feeling my shot nerves through the walls, and offers to lick my pussy just so I'll calm down.

"I can't be distracted!" I snap at him. His expression doesn't change much, never one to be affected by my attitude. It's one of the things I like most about him—his endurance for my mood swings.

The next thing I know, I'm being slammed against the wall opposite of where I can see the guests come through, with a hand wrapped tightly around my neck, and the other covering my mouth. Hot breath fans across my ear, sending shivers down my spine.

"Your pacing is going to attract attention if you don't fucking stop. I can hear you on the other side of the house," Mortis snaps harshly, his hand tightening around my throat until I can hardly breathe.

I wriggle against him, my anger rising like a wave in a storm. But the lust feels like a fucking tsunami. My chest heaves, though there's nowhere for the oxygen to go.

The hand on my mouth slides away from my face, past the valley between my breasts and down my nightgown. When he reaches the edge of my dress, he hitches up the bottom and pauses.

"Make another noise, and I'll tell the boys not to reward you with their cocks for a week, got it?"

I feel my face turning cherry red. Because there's nowhere for the blood in my head to go. Because of his audacity, and the threat. Because I can't fucking breathe. But mostly because I want him to fuck me already.

He lifts my head forward just to thump it harshly against the wall again. Hard enough for stars to glitter across my eyes and the little breath I had to escape. "Got it?" he repeats through bared teeth.

I nod my head, gritting my teeth against the storm of emotions swirling in my head.

"Good girl," he whispers, easing up on my throat a fraction, just enough for me to get a good deep breath before he tightens it again.

His fingers trail up my thigh, leaving a trail of goosebumps in its wake. The mere seconds it takes for his fingers to reach the juncture between my thighs feels like forever. But when the tips of his fingers whisper across my clit—my legs nearly give out. My knees tremble. If it wasn't for Mortis's hand wrapped firmly around my throat, I'd be a puddle of lust and cream on the floor.

"Fuck," he groans, dipping the tip of his middle finger in my pussy before spreading the cream up to my clit. "You're so fucking wet."

I open my mouth, but he thumps my head again before I can make a sound. "What did I just say? Not a single noise."

I clamp my mouth shut, tightening my lips into a thin line. As if that'll help. As if that'll actually stop the moan resting in my throat, growing by the second.

His finger presses into the sensitive bundle of nerves, swirling around and sending intense pleasure throughout my entire body. I grind my pussy harder against his hand, frantic for the sensations he's creating.

His finger circles faster against my clit. I struggle in his hold, desperately needing to breathe, but needing to come even more. His middle finger slides down to my opening and plunges deep inside me. I arch my back, and my eyes roll. His thumb continues the ministrations on my clit as he slips another finger inside me.

I'm fully gyrating into his hand now. My erratic movements cause the sharp talons on his fingers to dig into my throat. The sharp pinpricks heighten the agonizing bliss.

It takes a matter of moments for the coil in my stomach to snap and euphoria to render me boneless. I clamp my teeth down on my lips to keep quiet, squeezing my eyes shut tightly as I ride his hand, drawing out the orgasm crashing through me.

By the time I come down, Mortis has withdrawn his hand and I can breathe again. He keeps me upright now that my legs are jelly and useless against my weight. Small droplets of blood dot my dress, trailing from the tiny wounds on my neck, courtesy of Mortis's talons. The sight brings a smile to my face.

It's a wonder that he doesn't cut up the inside of my pussy, but he's always had perfect control of what he cuts.

Said talon pokes the underside of my chin, forcing my chin up until I'm looking into deep, soulful red eyes.

"You have the nose of a bloodhound. You're not going to miss any demons that come through this house," Mortis says, his tone a tad breathless, but stern.

I swallow and nod my head.

He kisses my lips softly, a stark contrast to his demeanor just minutes ago. Mortis may come off dry, but he's capable of so much more emotion than even he realizes.

His tongue licks the seam of my lips, and I grant him access. He explores my mouth thoroughly for a moment before he wrenches himself away. His cock is pressing against my stomach, but we both know we don't have time right now.

He has to get back to his post, and I need to keep an eye out for the demon.

Later. Later he will fuck me.

With one last kiss and a warning glance to stay calm, he walks away. Leaving me alone and breathless, but considerably calmer than before.

I smile, my heart filling with love and gratitude for my men. They know me better than I know myself most days.

I hear the front door open. My eyes focus and my spine snaps straight. Immediately, I make my way over to the peephole, pressing the entirety of my body against the wall.

A group of ten people stumble in, quickly pushing and shoving as they run to get away from the monsters. I breathe in deep but am disappointed when I don't detect any rot among the group of friends.

I slump, pressing my forehead against the wooden wall, ignoring flakes of sharp wood pricking against my skin. But I listen to Mortis, and stay calm.

Only a minute goes by when I hear the door open again. I lift my head slowly, confused by why another group would be entering the house.

We're at max capacity. The group hasn't even made it halfway yet. No one should be coming into this house yet.

As soon as the breeze wafts in from the open door, I get a whiff of something dreadful. Narrowing my eyes, I inhale deeply. Rot filters through my senses. A slow smile begins to form on my face and I feel any lingering frustration bleed out of me, replaced by excitement.

Walking into the house is a single guy, his head swiveling left and right as if he's searching for something. Or someone.

This naughty boy isn't supposed to be in this house. Excitement drums in my pulse.

Could it be Gary? It *has* to be. Why else would some guy sneak into a haunted house if he didn't have motive?

I cringe when I get a good look at the guy. God, he's really ugly—inside and out. A mop of greasy brown hair that's overgrown and curling past his bushy brows and ears. A dirty, threadbare hoodie hangs from his lanky body. I bet if I were to peek beneath the sleeves covering his arms, I'd find track marks and picked over scabs.

He's high. His pupils are dilated and shifty. Not from fear, but from whatever drug is coursing through his bloodstream. His cheeks have been hollowed out from the foreign substances eating away at this body from the inside out.

I've no idea what the hell Jennifer sees in this guy. He's so *gross*. And Jennifer is beautiful. With pretty, pin straight blonde hair, sky blue eyes and a radiating smile. How did someone like her end up with someone like *him?*

She must be fooled by the bad boy persona. Maybe she has a sad homelife, restricted from doing things that make her happy, so she's trying to find life and a thrill in someone dangerous. If only it means she feels a little less dead inside.

My flower is beginning to wilt, and just like Mommy, she will be tainted with tar if she stays with her vile boyfriend.

Gary's image flickers. I'm no longer staring at a greasy lowlife, but Daddy. Standing before me, looking straight into my eyes as if he can see me through the wall. A sinister smile growing on his portly face until all I can see, feel and hear is *evil.*

I gasp, jerking away as familiar terror claws through my bones. Every time Daddy walked into the same room as me, the oxygen was sucked out and replaced with fear. I was the only one that ever stood up to Daddy, but that doesn't mean I wasn't scared of him. That doesn't mean that I didn't fear for my life on a constant basis.

The image flickers, and Gary is before me again.

I let loose a harsh breath, shaking my hands out to calm the sharp nerves spearing through my body. I breathe in deeply, in through my nose and out through my mouth to calm the anxiety.

Breathe, Sibby. Daddy is dead. He's not here anymore.

This is why I'm here. *This* is my purpose. To protect my garden of flowers from wilting because of people like Gary and Daddy.

Gary pulls a gray beanie out of his hoodie pocket and pulls it over his head down low until his hair curls around the edges. His eyes travel across the foyer, noting the battery-operated woman giving birth to a demon on the couch—fake blood spurting from her orifices.

When he starts walking through the living room, the doll with the kitchen knife pops out from around the corner, cocking her head at Gary eerily and walking towards him.

"Stay the fuck back, you creepy bitch," Gary spits, venom in his voice. The girl stills, and for just a second, she breaks character as shock and fury flash across her eyes.

It's not very often we get aggressive guests. Afterall, the whole point of them being here is for them to chase after you and scare you.

The doll recovers quickly, a sinister smile building on her face as she continues her perusal. She has a job to do, and she's going to fucking do it. Don't enter the den of wolves and ask not to be bitten.

Gary scoffs. "Tell me which room Jennifer is in," he demands sharply. The doll ignores him, distracting him while another monster creeps up from behind him. A large man, nearly as big as Cronus, stands behind Gary.

Feeling the presence breathing down his neck, Gary turns and comes face-to-face with a monster that looks like a demonic man. Most of the skin is missing from his face, showing just the muscle beneath. The man is holding a chainsaw, and the second Gary lays eyes on him, the man revs the chainsaw, laughing manically as he does. Gary yells, his eyes dilating further, and he takes off up the stairs.

The opposite way he's supposed to go, but that's okay. He won't be lingering around for long.

I giggle, following him through the walls. I prance on my toes, keeping my footfalls light. I peek through each hole, keeping track of where he's going, laughing as the excitement of my kill builds.

He'll be so *cute* when he's ripped open, his lifeless eyes staring at me from between my thighs.

When he wanders in an empty room, I start to sing.

"Ring around the rosies."

Gary's head whips towards my voice, though he can't see me. His frantic eyes swivel around the room, ignoring the animated mannequin in the corner of the bedroom, stabbing itself with a knife brutally. Jackal is right outside of this room, having already scared Gary when he rushed in here.

Now that he's in here and Jackal has heard my singing, Gary will never come back out of the room.

"Pocket full of posies," I continue loudly. Jackal walks into the bedroom, his big yellow eyes locked on Gary. He checks the hallway one last time before shutting the door behind him. I swear his smile widens further the moment the door clicks shut. Gary whips around, jumping when he spots Jackal, his chest heaving.

He's not as unaffected by the monsters as he pretends to be. We're famous for a reason.

"The fuck do you want? I'm just trying to fucking find Jenny," he rages.

"Ashes, ashes."

Gary flinches from Jackal, his face painted in fear. It's such a beautiful sight, and it makes me squeal in excitement.

My henchman stalks towards Gary. His melted face and yellow eyes are a sight to behold. Sensing something is off, Gary begins to back away, searching left and right for an escape route. There are two doors in each room. The door our guests come through and the door they exit out of. The hallways and exits points aren't traditional to a real house, they're set up in an elaborate, but organized maze so each room will ultimately connect to the other.

Angling myself so I can see the exit point Gary is backing away towards, I smile when I see another one of my henchmen, Baine, appear behind him. The Grim Reaper, blocking his exit and sealing his death.

I bounce on my toes, giggling excitedly. How fun!

Gary doesn't notice him, though, too petrified of the melting monster before him. His chest heaves faster. His eyes are no longer dilated from the drugs, but from pure terror. Though I'm sure the drugs coursing through his system are intensifying the fear.

"What the fuck is going on?! Let me out of here!" Gary shouts, attempting to strong arm his way past Jackal. I almost snort, amused by his pathetic attempt. Gary is a tadpole compared to Jackal.

"We all fall down," I sing, drawing out the last note in a sorrowful tone. It seems as if the world stills, the three men on the other side of the wall pausing. And then they snap into action. Gary darts towards the door but Jackal catches him by his hood and shoves him back into the wall. The evil demon opens his mouth, preparing to let loose a scream, but Jackal's too fast. He shoves his hand over Gary's mouth, and punches him in the stomach with the other.

Gary loses his breath, hunching over from the pain. And just like that, Jackal brings his fist down on the back of Gary's head, knocking him out cold.

Gary slackens, his hunched body falling forward and crashing face-first to the dirty ground. I laugh when his body settles into a position where he's awkwardly on his knees, with his ass in the air and his face on the ground.

With excited giggles, I find my little hidden entrance and crawl through. The doors are only three feet tall. It's a little awkward to drag the demons through, but I usually don't have too much trouble.

Once I'm inside the room, I run up to Jackal, grab his face and bring him down to my level. I brush my lips against his softly, before deepening the kiss and plunging my tongue in his mouth. This time, I don't mind the fake, nasty blood on his mouth. Jackal groans, licking at my mouth eagerly. His cock hardens in his trousers, pressing against my stomach, the entirety of his body molding to mine.

I rip myself away from his mouth, panting and needy. As much as I'd love to pull down Jackal's pants, get on my knees and suck on his cock, I can't right now.

I have a job to do, and I need to hurry before more guests walk in.

Screams are sounding from all around the house. It's only a matter of time before I get caught.

After some maneuvering, I lift Gary up from underneath his arms and drag him towards the door.

I'm a lot stronger than most would give me credit for. My height doesn't crest past five-five, but I've always insisted on carrying the demons once they've been knocked out. Most of the time, I'm the one doing the knocking out.

My henchmen will do anything for me, but I like to take care of them myself. They risk enough for me. If anyone ever walks in on us, it'll be me dragging them off into the depths of this house—not them.

It takes me thirty seconds to drag him up to the small door, crawl in and then drag his body in after me. I shut the door, pick him back up and drag him off towards the stairs. Just as the door shuts behind me, a group of people bursts into the room, screams still trapped on their tongues. I leave my men to their jobs while I wrangle Gary down the hallway. There's a small alcove by the stairs big enough to fit a small group of people.

I work quickly, having learnt my lesson already. There's been a time or two where they've woken up in the middle of me tying them up, and it was *so* annoying to knock them out again. Ropes are stashed behind the stairs, ready for when I bring a demon back here.

I tie each of his legs to the wooden chair leg in an intricate knot. It took me a bit, but after the first year in Satan's Affair, I mastered tying a knot so well—they had no chance of escape. I tie his arms behind the chair's back, and then I pin his torso to the chair by wrapping a larger rope around his chest.

His head lolls and drool gathers in the corner of his mouth. Soon, it'll start trailing out. Curling my lip in disgust, I grab my roll of duct tape, tear off a strip and slap it on his acne-ridden face. His screams won't be completely silent, but they'll be muffled enough that they'll be swallowed up by the other screams going on around the house.

No one has ever heard a demon calling for help in my house. And they never fucking will.

I bound off towards the room I know Jennifer is working in. I want to stay close to her to make sure she's doing okay. I don't know her, nor does she even know of my existence, but I feel the need to comfort her. So badly, I want to tell her that I'm taking care of her—that she no longer has to worry about her rapist.

He's getting exactly what he deserves.

After I extinguish her shitty boyfriend—I know in my heart she's going to heal and find someone better. How could she not know that the soul-sucking leech has been ripped from her body and soul?

I find her in my playroom, hiding under the bed. Once a group arrives, she'll crawl out from under the bed, her limbs distorted as she chases after them. I overheard her saying before she used to be a gymnast. No one does this job better than her.

We wait for a few minutes before we hear a loud group coming down the hallway. I press myself against the peephole, keeping my eye on the space Jennifer is going to crawl out of.

The group barrels in the room, stumbling like a bunch of drunk fools as they scream and push each other to get away from the monster chasing after them with a chainsaw. They're guaranteed to come in this room since Jackal is posted up at the end of the hallway, keeping anyone from wanting to come near him.

On cue, Jennifer's distorted body comes crawling out from under the bed. A redheaded girl screams, the pitch of it making me cringe away from the wall.

That was fucking obnoxious.

Good thing she smells like petunias or I'd kill her.

The group of girls push and shove at each other as they run towards the exit, avoiding Jennifer like the plague. They fling up the other door, the wood bounding off the stopper. If there wasn't one, the wall would have a permanent imprint of the door in the cheap drywall from how hard people open the door.

Once they're out, Jennifer gets up and softly closes the doors again. Her face is hidden from view as she does, her movements slow. I hold my breath, hoping to see her normal happy face. But when she finally turns, tears are gathered in her lids.

I frown, my heart dropping.

Why is she crying? I saved her! She should be rejoicing.

She sniffles, carefully wiping her eyes before the tears fall and ruin her makeup.

Is she... she couldn't possibly be upset that her boyfriend didn't show up? He raped her! How could she be upset over something like that?

I snarl, her ungratefulness releasing a black cloud of ink inside me. I made sure her rapist didn't come near her. He would've only hurt her if he did. He would've spun her back into his web again, and she would've fallen victim to a black widow that would slowly poison her until nothing good is left.

Until her flower is wilted.

I stay by the wall for hours, watching Jennifer's attitude increasingly decline as the night goes on. Every time I see a tear drop from her eye, I see Mommy before me, crying into her hands as Daddy punishes her.

The second the last guests of the night leave her room, she sits on the bed and sobs. Holding her face in her hands like a small child, black tears trailing down her cheeks from her makeup.

I reach toward her, but the wall hinders me.

"Mommy?" I whisper. Jennifer's blonde hair bleeds to Mommy's dark brown hair, and all I can see is a woman sobbing her heart out, praying for death. And then her blonde hair is back, and I can't tell if the lone tear that trails down my cheek is for Jennifer or Mommy.

It doesn't take long for Sarah to come looking for her. The second she sees Jennifer's state, she sits on the bed next to her and cocoons the weeping girl in her arms.

"What's wrong? Did he come see you?"

Jennifer drops her arms and wails, "That's just the thing! He didn't show up."

I can only see their backs, but Sarah's silence is weighted.

"I... thought that's what you wanted," Sarah hedges, her tone tight with confusion.

Jennifer wipes her eyes and gives a pitiful shrug. "I wanted to see what he would say, but as usual, he's fucking unreliable and always lies. He's probably out doing drugs again. He said he stopped that, but I don't think he did."

I scowl. He definitely didn't.

"Didn't you tell him you didn't want to see him?"

Jennifer scoffs, "Yeah, so? If he really cared about me, he would've shown up and at least tried to explain himself."

Another weighted silence passes. Sarah sees that Jennifer is in a toxic cycle. Despite what Gary did to her, she was still hoping he'd show up. And because I stopped that from happening, she's pissed.

The black ink spreads deeper inside of me.

What an ungrateful bitch! My hand trembles as rage consumes me. I work hard to rid this world of evil. Gary would've met the same fate regardless—I would've smelled his stench from the first step inside my house. But I probably wouldn't have bothered to lure him away until after he talked to Jennifer.

I *saved* her.

It seems I made a mistake in doing so.

Snarling, I rip away from the wall and stalk back towards Gary. I'm feeling particularly savage. God help the souls that will feel my wrath.

Chapter 5

Gary's awake.

Tears leak from wide eyes as he struggles in his bonds. Blood leaks from where the rope is rubbing his skin raw.

When he lays eyes on me, he screams with all his might. The sound is less significant than a kitten's cry.

I giggle behind my hand, amused by his distress. Seeing him fight his bonds with renewed tears eases some of the anger in my chest.

His shouting continues, and it sounds like he's trying to curse at me. Muffled words and empty threats, that's all I hear.

Despite his girlfriend's ungratefulness, what he did to her was wrong. Sick. Depraved. Only something someone with a rotten soul would do. And he deserves to die for it.

There's no redemption for people like Gary. They never learn their lesson. They get a slap on the wrist and then go on with their lives, torturing women for the sake of inflating their self-worth. Truth is, they don't have any worth, and they know that.

They're lost souls, wandering the Earth, searching for something they will never find.

I crouch in front of him, cocking my head and giving him a wide smile.

"We are going to have so much fun together," I say reverently, already picturing all the places I'm going to slice and stab. Maybe I'll paint a pretty picture with his blood when I'm done.

Oh! I wonder if Jennifer would like that. Maybe *then* she'll appreciate what I did for her.

His screams and wriggling intensify. He nearly topples the chair over from his struggles. If he does, I'm going to be really annoyed.

"Do you know Jennifer?" I ask innocently. At the sound of his girlfriend's name, he stills. His bottomless brown eyes heat as his chest heaves. He says something, and I don't bother to rip off the tape to hear what he said. I'm not ready for him to talk back yet. "Did you know you hurt her?" I ask.

His brows plunge, and he shoots me a nasty look. I forge on, "She was crying to her friend today. About how you raped her when she was inebriated. Too drunk to stop you. But she said she did try. She told you no and you didn't listen. That's called rape, Gary."

He shouts something again. It sounded like he said something along the lines of, "She's my girlfriend."

I nod my head slowly, looking him up and down in disgust. "She *is* your girlfriend. But that doesn't mean you have the right to do what you want to her body without her consent. Last time I checked, it's not *your* body."

More muffles come from his mouth that I don't care to decipher. I slap his cheek—hard. His eyes widen in shock and rage, looking at me as if he can't believe I just slapped him.

Oh, Gary. I'm going to do so much worse to you.

"You're not in the position to argue," I hiss.

He quiets, the anger receding as fear bleeds back into his irises. Good. That's what

I like to see.

I spin and trek through the hallways, checking each room to make sure they're empty. The fair shut down for the night, but sometimes employees linger. The last thing I need is to bring Gary out and someone stumble upon him. Then I'd have to commit the ultimate sin and kill an innocent person. I would go to Hell for it, and I'd accept that punishment if it meant I could continue my life's work.

Once I confirm me and my henchmen are well and truly alone, I calmly walk behind a squirming Gary, press my thumb into the pressure point in his neck and increase the pressure until he's once more slumping in his seat. After untying his bonds and dragging him out to the middle of the foyer, I walk away.

It's always my favorite part when they think they have a chance of escape. To see the hope slowly fade out of their eyes when they realize there's no chance of them getting past my henchmen.

I make my way into my playroom, sit crisscross-applesauce on the floor and wait with a smile on my face. My pretty knife rests loosely in my hand. While I wait, I hold the knife to the light. It glints off my blade, turning the dull metal into a pretty sparkle.

The only thing that would make this prettier is bright red blood dripping off of it.

I giggle to myself. Soon. So, so soon.

It takes all of ten minutes before I hear a thump from somewhere downstairs. Mortis stands in the corner of the room, his face slack and bored as usual. He doesn't move an inch from where he stands, just like a loyal little henchman. He won't move until I tell him to.

"Let me out!" comes a muffled shout from below. I'm sure he's currently shouting in one of my henchmen's faces. Plenty of the demons try to fight them, but they always ended up getting knocked down anyways. My henchmen don't kill the demons—they leave that to me. But they do enjoy hurting them.

"Ring around the rosies, pocket full of posies," I sing, making sure my voice is nice and loud. Another thump, followed by a growl of frustration. Eventually, when the demons get tired of trying to make their way through my henchmen, they come to me, pleading for escape. Some try to kill me even.

"Ashes, ashes, we all fall down!" I end the song on a shout, giddiness taking over.

"You fucking bitch!" Gary shouts again, pounding on something as he does. I hope he doesn't start destroying shit. It took Mortis all night to repair the wall from the last guy who took an axe to the wall.

Finally, I hear his loud footsteps coming up the stairs. He'll make his way in and out of the maze of rooms before he finds himself in the hallway outside of my playroom, with Jackal standing at the end of the hall.

And just like the guests, he'll want to avoid Jackal, so he'll come into my room. I smile when Gary comes barreling into the room, chest pumping a mile a minute and a pissed off expression on his ugly face.

He'll look so much prettier after I rip it apart. Maybe peel the nasty flesh from his face.

"What. The. Fuck. Is. Wrong with you?!" he shouts, spittle flying from his rotted mouth. My smile grows when I get a glimpse of blackened teeth. Whether it's from the drugs or his soul doesn't matter. He's going to die either way.

I stand slowly, a serene smile plastered on my made-up face.

He charges at me, a loud shout ringing from his mouth. I easily side-step, watching as he catches wind and falls face first onto the ground. I giggle, covering my mouth with my hand. He struggles to get back up again, disoriented and probably coming down from his high by now.

Another giggle escapes when he stumbles as he rights himself. Fiery pits full of poison peer up at me. His eyes—they're forged straight from Hell. I've cast my judgement and I've made the right call.

"I will fucking kill you," he fumes, his voice having darkened to a low, deep pitch.

I snicker. "Not if I kill you first," I sing. He growls and charges again. I time it exactly right, swiping out my hand so the tip of the blade glides across his eye. The cornea of his eye rips away from the pupil, the thin piece dangling on the tip of my knife.

Gary covers his eye, crying out in rage. His voice cracks as blood trails down his cheek. I do love it when they cry blood. Taking advantage of his distraction, I stab the knife into his stomach. He hunches over on a pained yelp, coughing up blood.

Bliss builds in my chest. I retract the knife and plunge into his flesh again, the blade tearing past meat and sinew. The demon gurgles, getting his putrid blood all over me. I push him back, and the pathetic sack of flesh falls backwards. Dropping the blade, I grab my handsaw from the bed.

When he sees what's in my hand, his eyes widen.

"No, no, no," he pleads, crawling backwards. I lift my foot and stomp on his ankle. It takes a few more stomps before I hear the bone crack. Screams fill the air. Gary's hands clutch at his foot, staring at it in disbelief.

"Don't be so dramatic, I'm sure I only fractured it."

"What the fuck is wrong with you?!" he shouts, turning his glare back to me. I kick his head back as a response. When he falls back, I step on his chest, pin one arm down and begin sawing at his flesh. Slicing through skin and meat is easy, it's when you get to the bone that it gets a little hard.

Gary struggles beneath me, further ripping the tendons and veins apart. I jerk down on the handle, cracking through the bone as I continue to saw. Blood spurts wildly, splattering all over me, the bed and the floor. Good thing haunted houses are filled with fake blood.

Even if my henchmen miss a few spots when they clean up, no one will ever be able to tell the difference.

I twist the limb, detaching it the rest of the way from the tendons.

Gary's a screamer. I giggle, enjoying the shock and outrage on his face as he stares at his missing arm. I offer the bloody limb to him.

"You want to bite down on it for the next arm?" His eyes slide to me, the pupils nearly gone. Funny how he came in with blown out pupils and now they're tiny little pinpricks in the whites of his eyes.

"Fuck you," he pants breathlessly. I smile and chuck the arm to the side.

"Fine," I chirp, stepping back over him. I grab his hand and saw off each of his fingers. The little demon won't be able to damage the walls like that last one.

"See, Mortis? I'm learning!" I exclaim, pointing at the chopped-up man.

Mortis offers a small smile and a nod. He doesn't show emotion much, but the

51

gleam in his eye tells me he's amused.

"Good job, baby girl," he murmurs.

With a wide smile, I turn back to Gary. A missing arm, no fingers on his other, and a fractured foot.

I really want to watch him run away. But first, I need to cauterize his wound, otherwise he'll continue to lose blood too quickly, and then we won't get to play. I keep a mini blowtorch stashed in one of the end tables for this purpose.

Hurrying over to grab the torch, I snatch it out of the pink drawer and then crouch in front of Gary.

"You ready?" I ask. He looks at me like I'm insane.

That hurts my feelings.

So, I click the button, grinning at the blue fire that erupts from it. When Gary sees the flame, his eyes widen and he goes to get up. I crawl on top of him, sitting on his stomach and quickly bring the flame to where his arm once was attached.

Screams spill from his mouth in piercing waves. The smell of charred human flesh and meat fill the air. I scrunch my nose, repulsed by the smell. Demons smell like shit.

He squirms desperately beneath me as I make quick work of cauterizing the wound.

"There!" I announce proudly, clicking off the flame. "Now we can play a little longer."

I stand and step back, watching the demon thrash and moan, still riding the waves of his wound being sealed shut. Sweat floods from his pores, stinking up the room even further.

"Quit being a baby," I whine, exasperated. When he continues to complain, I grit through my teeth, "Get up!"

His eyes snap to me. "Go on," I urge impatiently. "Try to escape."

Why do all the demons look at me like I'm crazy when I tell them to run? They always think I'm tricking them when I'm very serious. I love when they run. True, they won't ever escape. But I'm only telling them to *try*. Whether they're successful is totally out of their hands.

With great pain and even greater slowness, Gary rolls to sit up.

"How the fuck do you expect me to run, you crazy ass bitch?" he snarls at me, looking hopelessly at his foot. He looks like he's on the verge of passing out. A greyish pallor has bleached his skin.

Well. The skin that's *not* covered in his blood.

Pretty soon, he'll pass out. Which is exactly why he needs to run. The hope of escape will get his adrenaline rushing again. It'll keep him conscious long enough for me to have more fun with him before I end his life.

"Get up!" I screech, stomping my foot. I hate when they don't listen! He startles, looking at me with the same expression. Like *I'm* the crazy one when he's the one with an evil soul.

He maneuvers onto his knee and uses his good foot to push off the ground. Sweat continues to pour from his face and drips into his eye. He squeezes them shut, probably to abate the sting from sweat mixing into an eye with a missing cornea. Gritting his teeth, he takes his first step. And immediately falls back down. Looks like he's not scared enough.

"If you don't run in fifteen seconds, I will remove one of your eyeballs," I threaten. I'll do it, too.

He glares at me and spits at my feet.

I gasp and step back. Curling my lip, I consider how to get him up.

"If you can get up and open one of the doors, I'll let you go."

Finally, hope trickles back into his eyes. The pain was overbearing, and he started to give up. He just needed a little nudge to get going.

"Ring around the rosies," I sing, taking on the child-like haunting voice. His movements quicken, and soon enough, he's back on his feet and limping down the hallway. Broken foot be damned.

Giddiness overtakes me. I bounce on my feet, giving him a good head start. He'll be laughably easy to catch. I don't want it to be over too soon.

"Pocket full of posies."

Several crashes followed by loud cursing. He fell down the stairs. I laugh loudly and run out of the room and make my way to the stairs. He's at the bottom, groaning in pain as he struggles to get up. When he spots me, his eyes widen and he resumes his struggles with renewed energy.

Colorful curses slither from his mouth as he gets back up on his feet and turns towards the front door. Cronus is standing there, completely still as he watches Gary.

"What is wrong with you? I thought you wanted me to run?!" he shouts. Cronus doesn't react. I tiptoe down the stairs, stopping halfway down.

"I said you have to open the door," I clarify. He doesn't turn to acknowledge me, the scary man before him stealing all his attention and fear. But he does listen. He barrels towards Cronus, shoves him aside, bends and bites onto the handle.

I giggle, amused by how cute he looks trying to open a door with his mouth. For a solid minute, I let him struggle to open the door with his teeth. He then switches tactics, balancing on his good foot while using his knee and fingerless hand to clutch the handle. He wobbles and falls before he can make any progress. He's lost too much blood and is becoming weaker.

"Here I come," I taunt, coming further down the stairs.

Snarling, he whips away from the door and drags himself down the hallway, leaning his shoulder against the wall for support. Quickly, I descend the rest of the stairs and watch as he painstakingly makes his way into the kitchen. He glances back at me, his eyes rounding when he sees me standing there.

He'll be sorely disappointed when he finds Baine or Timothy at the other exit point.

Green and purple smoke unfurls from the machines in the corners, thickening in the hallway. Gary disappears, his torn apart body swallowed by the smoke and flashing strobe lights. I can hear his grunts and curses.

At one point, I hear a sharp crack, followed by a loud shout from Gary. I'm pretty sure his foot just broke further. I run through the living room and around to the kitchen, coming through a side entrance. Off to the side of the kitchen is a tiny foyer with a staircase and the only other exit. When guests are finished upstairs, they come down that staircase and exit through the door. Standing guard in front of the foyer is Baine—my little grim reaper.

That's who he's dressed up as, with his black hooded cloak and skeletal body. He puts Mortis's body to shame, with the entirety of his rib cage poking through his grey-painted skin. Along with every other bone in his body. He says he doesn't like to eat, and I don't push him to correct his eating disorder. His cock is skinny but is the longest out of the bunch so he always gets to fuck my ass.

"Motherfucking, BITCH!"

I slap a hand over my mouth as more cackles release from my mouth.

Gary's head drops, hopelessness seeming to consume him. His shoulders shudder as a sob wracks his throat. My hand falls and I walk closer, getting a full view of him. Tears stream down his bloodied face, producing pretty pink tears that drip off his face and onto the floor.

"Just fucking kill me," he sobs. He sways, losing all fight and nearly collapsing to the floor. His body jolts as he cries, and finally, it folds in on itself and he falls to the ground. His sobs deepen, while Baine and I share a look.

How pathetic. Raping and abusing women and when he's abused in return, it's one big pity party.

"Are you going to admit to your sins?" I ask, stepping closer and leaning down, putting my face directly into his.

"What sins?" he blubbers, snot leaking into his mouth.

I slap him, my own hand stinging from the impact. "Don't play stupid! What did you do to, Jennifer?" I interrogate, curling my lip over my teeth.

"I...I had sex with her."

Apparently, his ears stopped working. I grip my knife and plunge it into his stomach. He gasps, blood mixing into his saliva as he coughs.

"I'll ask again," I say serenely. "What did you do to her?"

He sniffles. "I raped her," he confesses on a pitiful cry. "She was my girlfriend! I didn't think it was that big of a deal!"

My eyes widen as a thick film of red-hot rage contorts my vision.

"Not a big deal?" I whisper, shocked by his words.

He stutters, not managing to get a coherent sentence out when he knows he just fucked up. I'm sure he can see it in my face. The absolute stupidity of what he just uttered.

My spine straightens and a calm smile settles on my face.

His words only justify my judgement. Every time I'm proved right, I'm overcome with peace. Breathing out a sigh, I turn and go find my Mace—a long, skinny wooden bat covered in spikes. Normally, it's used as a prop. Jackal will carry it in his hand sometimes. What no one knows, is that it's real. The spikes aren't plastic, but a sharpened metal.

When I return to Gary, he's still on the floor throwing his pity party. I know it's going to get uglier once he lays eyes on what's in my hand. Like clockwork, his eyes bulge and he starts desperately chanting to me.

"No, no, no, please, no," he wails, tears streaming down his reddened face. I suppose it's better than the grey.

He still looks like shit, though.

Baine steps closer, his eyes watching intently as I bring the Mace down on his other foot, ensuring no escape from Gary. He screams, his face turning cherry red. His foot is nearly detached from his leg. Blood leaks out in rivulets from the pulpy mess his ankle now is.

Baine fists his cock, the muscle hard and straining beneath his black robe. I smile, feeling my own desire building in the apex of my thighs.

My henchmen were *made* for me. Each and every one of them.

Deftly, I unbuckle Gary's belt and pull down his pants. He wriggles, trying his best to dislodge my hands, but he only succeeds in getting them down quicker.

"What are you doing?!" he shouts, panicked.

His boxers come down next, and I nearly gag from the stench.

"Gary. Do you ever wash your ass?" I ask seriously, my face curled with repulsion. I mean, *really*, when's the last time this filthy parasite even showered?

I will never understand what Jennifer sees in him. There's no way she has rose-colored glasses on with him. She has dark, black sunshades on. It's the only way she can look at Gary and not see something revolting.

Curses are spit at me, but I ignore them. They're just empty words. How can they mean anything at all when they're coming from the mouth of a demon?

"You said what you did to Jennifer wasn't a big deal," I reiterate. Thrashing desperately, he doesn't answer. He knows what's coming.

Baine does, too. His robe has been pulled aside, and in his tightly curled fist, he pumps his cock. Gary pays him no mind, his terror too potent to pay attention to the grim reaper jacking off over his head.

"If you don't feel raping an innocent flower isn't *a big deal*, then I will do you the same honor. Shouldn't be a big deal, right?" I say, flipping him on his stomach. He looks like a squirming leech.

I squeal with laughter when he starts hyperventilating. "I take it back! I take it back!"

His ass stinks, but it's a small price to pay. I don't even bother spreading his flat cheeks. The business end of the Mace is positioned right at his ass, and I shove upwards.

It doesn't just slide in, though. It takes work and maneuvering.

"Stop! Please, *please stop!*" I don't listen. I keep shoving until the Mace finally slithers into his ass. Blood spurts from the wound as I fuck Gary's ass with the spiked weapon.

"No big deal, right, Gary?" I scream over his shouting, my voice nearly hysteric. I slide the Mace in and out, shivering in delight from the noises his body makes as its ripped apart.

Baine jerks his dick faster, his chin to his chest as he watches the scene with unveiled enchantment. Groans slip from his throat, and soon, cum spurts from his dick, landing on the floor and mixing it with Gary's blood.

I laugh, though Gary hasn't even noticed due to his entrails being dragged out from his ass. I drag the bat out, his intestines wrapped around the spikes, and other parts of his innards.

Gary convulses as his entrails slide out of him. Within seconds, his screaming ceases and silence settles over the house. All that's left is my heavy breathing.

My eyes land on Baine's bottomless eyes.

"Get the others over here. Now."

Chapter 6

My pulse drums with excitement as I strip from my bloodied nightgown and slippers. Timothy slinks out from the depths of the house, his glorious body on display. He stops short when he spots Gary and the mess I made. And then his gaze slides to me, my naked body covered in blood.

"Do you want me to clean it, Sibby?" he asks, his deep voice laced with excitement.

I smile gleefully. "Not yet."

Jackal and Mortis appear, each of their eyes filled with hunger, eating up the entirety of my naked body. Jackal licks his bloody lips, eager to do what his eyes are conveying. He looks as if he already ripped someone apart with his teeth, and now I want him to do the same to me.

Cronus comes in behind them, and though I can't see his mouth and eyes beneath the prosthetics, his body vibrates with need.

Baine comes back into the room last. He's the ghost of the house—always out of sight until his presence is absolutely necessary.

Heat gathers between my thighs as my boys gather around me. Ravenous and hungry for me, just as I always am for them.

An ornate wooden dining room table is in the corner of the kitchen and sitting in each chair are mannequins—their flesh ripped from their faces and mouths open. Utensils are gripped in their hands as another fake dead body is in the middle of the table, its chest flayed open. Parts of the fake human are on the plates resting in front of each cannibalistic mannequin, ready to be eaten.

Sliding out one of the chairs and setting aside the grotesque dummy, Mortis sits down on the chair. He loves to watch first, stroking his dick gently as to not come too quickly.

"Cronus, baby, will you put that dead body somewhere?" I ask, pointing at the flayed open mannequin. Cronus heeds my request, pulling out the chairs and pushing them to the side, and then dragging the mannequin off the table.

Eagerly, I crawl on top of the table, my ass facing them as I arch my back and lower the upper half of my body to the cool wood. My nipples tighten the second the cool wood presses against them.

Timothy grabs my hips, pulling me towards him so my knees are balanced precariously on the edge. He then turns away from me and crouches on the floor, his back pressed to the edge of the table as he leans his head all the way back onto the table, in between my legs. Reaching up, he grabs my hips once more and lowers me onto his face, his long tongue snaking out and licking the entirety of my pussy.

A breathless moan escapes, and my eyes roll as his tongue explores me. Jackal steps over Timothy, his cock firmly in his grip as he guides the tip to my entrance. I look back at Jackal and smile as the fake blood drips from his mouth and onto the flesh of my ass. His burnt fingers swipe at the blood, mixing the fake with the real.

He doesn't break eye contact as he plunges inside of me, his yellow eyes bright with desire. My mouth drops, the sensations immediately sending shudders through me. Jackal's head tips back, and a long, but quiet groan releases from his throat. He's always so quiet, but his presence is the loudest.

His chin drops, connecting his eyes with mine once more as he creates a steady rhythm. My mouth stays open, letting loose small moans that I couldn't stop if I tried. Cronus hurries onto the table, coming around to kneel in front of me. I lift my head and instantly open my mouth. I glimpse his thick, veiny dick before it's shoved in my mouth, nearly choking me on his length. I moan around his cock, but my mouth is too full for the sound to escape.

Just like they want.

Timothy's tongue flicks my clit as he sucks and licks. I reach down and yank on tufts of his blue hair, receiving an answering groan that vibrates against my pussy. Pure bliss radiates from where his tongue is swiping at the bundle of sensitive nerves, and where Jackal's cock is sliding in and out of me. Drool forms in the corners of my mouth as my legs tremble from the intense pleasure radiating from my core.

Baine climbs onto the table next, straddling my body with his feet planted firmly on the wooden surface. He slowly backs up, while Jackal leans away, making room for Baine as he continues to fuck me. Jackal pulls out long enough to allow Baine to plunge the entirety of his cock inside me, coating himself in my juices. He pulls out and Jackal resumes, pounding into me with renewed ferocity.

Baine grabs my hip with one hand, guides his cock with the other until the tip is crowning my tight hole. I squeeze my eyes shut, trembling from the pleasure and the pain I know is coming. In one thrust, Baine seats himself completely inside me. A scream ripples around Cronus's dick. He jerks in my mouth and a breathy groan releases from his throat.

"You're so fucking tight," Baine murmurs, his words dipped in sin. "Covered in blood, looking like a fucking goddess of death."

"She tastes so good too," Timothy sighs around my center, nearly grinding his lips against me.

Baine doesn't give me a moment to adjust. His hips slam into me, jolting me forward and causing Jackal to slip from my pussy. Pain consumes my backside, fire licking at the edges of my not-so-forbidden entrance. He slowly glides out, and slams into me again. He repeats this process, until the pain recedes and pleasure slides into place. When I arch back into Baine, Jackal slaps the tip of his cock against my entrance, teasing me.

I rear my head back enough to allow Cronus's cock to slip free. Long enough to demand, "Fuck me, Jackal. I need it so bad."

Jackal releases a guttural growl, deep in his chest as he acquiesces, slamming back inside me. His hips quicken, and my muscles turn to jelly. Cronus wraps his hand around the back of my head and pumps his hips, the swollen head slipping far down my throat and depleting the oxygen from my lungs. I suck and lick at his engorged flesh, roving my tongue alongside the thick vein pulsing in my mouth. Drool slips from my mouth, creating a pool of saliva below me, but I don't care.

I look up at him, and now more than ever I wish the prosthetics weren't covering his eyes and mouth. I want to see his mouth propped open by his hunger for me, and his eyes staring down at me as he watches me suck his cock.

His veiny hand squeezes my hair, while the other reaches up to caress my face. His fingers dragging over my skin reverently, communicating that he loves what I'm doing to him in the only way he can.

Euphoria builds in my pussy, gathering and swirling until it overwhelms my entire being. My stomach dips, becoming impossibly tight until it feels like a rubber band being pulled too tight. Timothy's tongue swirls over my clit in just the perfect way, and I can no longer hold on.

The rubber band snaps, and I fall over the cliff. My eyes widen as intense pleasure rolls through my body, stealing my breath from my lungs. I go blind, blackness stealing my vision as I ride out the waves rolling through me. My pussy grinds against Timothy's face uncontrollably as Jackal and Baine drill harder into me.

I feel, rather than hear, Mortis climb onto the table. He pets my hair, leaning down to whisper in my ear.

"Shh, Sibby. You have to be quiet," Mortis demands quietly, eliciting shivers from the base of my neck down to my spine. I gurgle around Cronus's dick, an attempt at whining.

I don't *have* to do anything. If no one heard Gary's screams, then surely they won't hear me.

"Let me get under her," Mortis says. Timothy moves out from under me, and Jackal and Baine slide out. Mortis slides beneath me, grabbing my thighs and settling them on either side of him. I let Cronus's cock slip from my lips, already feeling so incredibly empty.

Mortis loves me on top. It's his favored position and one I'm also happy to oblige. Biting my lip to contain a wide smile, I slide the crown of Mortis's cock up and down my sopping pussy. He groans, low in his throat, his red eyes shining with dark promises.

"Sit on my fucking cock, Sibby. Now."

I'm eager to comply. I slide his tip to my opening and slam my hips down. Cronus doesn't waste time, slipping his cock past my lips to keep the moan from spilling out. Jackal and Baine move back into their positions. Slowly, Jackal works his cock into my pussy alongside Mortis's, filling me so full that I can hardly breathe. I'll never get used to the feeling of two dicks inside one hole—it feels too fucking good.

Once Jackal is in position, Baine follows suit and slides back inside my ass.

I squeeze my eyes shut, so tightly that I see stars.

"I wanna feel this pussy drenching me with your cum," Mortis says right before lifting his head and drawing Cronus's balls in his mouth. Cronus's head kicks back, the veins in his throat pulsing as he barely holds onto the roar threatening to rip from his mouth.

All at once, my men begin to fuck me. Drilling their cocks into me until I don't know where they begin and I end.

"Fuck, Timmy," Jackal grunts from behind me. I smile around Cronus, knowing Timothy is sliding his cock right into Jackal's ass. More than anything, I want to watch Timothy fuck Jackal, but I can't bear to stop sucking on Cronus.

Pressure begins to build again as my henchmen pump their hips frantically. The sound of skin slapping and heavy breathing fills the room. Hands grab at me desperately, though the blood coating my body makes it hard for them to get a firm grip. The thought sends a fresh wave of pleasure straight to my core.

I lose all control over my body, slumping against Mortis. Cronus wraps his hand around my throat, keeping my head up as he fucks my mouth. The veins beneath his skin bulge, and the sight of his power makes my knees tremble. His hand squeezes tighter and tighter, until I can no longer breathe with his engorged dick ravishing my mouth.

Tears prick at my eyes and black spots dot my vision.

I need to breathe, but I need to come even more.

My men's thrusts become sloppy and erratic as our orgasms build. Cronus reaches his peak first, groaning long and low as hot cum spurts from his cock. My mouth fills, and he releases the tension around my throat just enough for my cheeks to puff out. I have to focus on swallowing.

Cronus slides out, allowing the guttural screams from my throat to finally be heard. I come harder than I ever have before, my pussy gripping my men impossibly tight. I scream and scream, not caring if I'm heard two towns over.

Jackal and Baine follow suit a few seconds before Mortis. Judging by Timothy's loud groan, I assume he found his release, too.

It feels like gallons of semen are being spilled into my body. My tummy bloats from the amount, and I have to grind my teeth against the incredible fullness.

And like a hand being pulled from a puppet, we all collapse, our bodies languid and shaky.

My head rolls to the side, my cheek smashed against Mortis's bony shoulder. Blood smears across my cheek, but I don't have the energy to care.

I stare at Gary. What's left of him at least. It looks as if a powerful vacuum attached itself to his mouth and sucked the life out of him.

A tired smile draws across my face as peace settles deep within. I did something good today. Another evil soul, ridden from this planet.

Mortis taps my shoulder lightly. With a harrumph, I roll off of him. Him and the boys pick themselves up and start cleaning up the mess I made. Timothy cleans the blood, while Mortis drags Gary's body out of the house. Jackal leaves to go find the stray body parts and clean upstairs.

"How do you feel?" Baine asks, his voice barely above a whisper. He talks like he's a ghost.

"Good," I sigh.

"Tomorrow morning we leave for Seattle, Washington. I heard rumors about that area."

My brow puckers.

"What rumors?" I ask softly, watching as Jackal walks out of the room with a hand full of fingers and an arm.

"A massive pedophile ring is there. A lot of politicians and celebrities hang around there."

My eyes widen. It blows my mind that these things actually happen. I can't understand how people could kidnap and rape boys and girls. Little innocent babies to teenagers. And then sell them and torture them in the worst imaginable ways. Sparks of anger ignite, my mind wandering to all the horrific things they probably do to those poor souls. Poor, innocent souls. Only a truly evil person could do something like that to a child. A *baby*.

Only demons could do that.

"I'm hoping some of them come through Satan's Affair," I say aloud. Then, "What if more than one come through?" I muse. Surprisingly, that hasn't happened yet. More than one evil soul coming through my house at once. "How would I choose?"

Baine is silent for a moment. His bony, white fingers drift over my skin, eliciting goosebumps from my flesh. I shiver beneath his touch. His fingers trail across my stomach.

"Who says you have to choose? Kill them all, Sibby."

Chapter 7

about eighteen
years old

I

t took eight days, sixteen hours, twenty-four minutes and thirteen seconds for Mommy to come back.

She walked into our shared bedroom, looking no worse for wear. Her brown hair hangs limp around her shoulders, stringy and threadbare. Her dull brown eyes as lifeless as they've always been. Mommy was always been skinny, but as the years pass by, her body grows frailer and her bones curve, like she's retreating in on herself.

Sometimes I wonder if she ever looked at me with love in her eyes when I was born. Before Daddy sucked her lifeforce away. What did she look like before him? Was she vibrant and full of life and love? Did she do everything with passion and ferocity?

I want to know who she was before she let someone destroy her so deeply.

"Mommy!" I gasp, rushing to her and embracing her in a loose hold.

I learned long ago not to hold her too tightly. It hurts her.

Relief washes through me so strongly, it takes all I have not to collapse from the force of it.

"I'm okay, sweetie," she says tonelessly, patting my back before stepping away. She ambles past me, her slippers sliding against the floor as she walks.

Did she pick up her feet when she walked before Daddy came into her life?

"What happened to you?" I ask, following after her like a lost puppy.

She glances at me, but her eyes shift constantly, never staying in one place for more than a second. Never looking directly at me. Another thing that's shifting throughout the years—it seems to get harder and harder for her to meet my eyes.

"I was in one of the other houses," she replies.

Daddy created a small compound for the Church to live in. He came from a long line of old money, so he bought a hundred acres of land and built ten large houses, all set up in a square. He assigns a couple of the trusted Church goers to go outside the compound and get whatever supplies we need once a month.

Otherwise, none of us are allowed outside the premise. Especially without his permission. We go to school every day with one teacher, and then do work around the house to keep us busy.

When a man has eighteen kids, with five more on the way, it's important to implement some type of law and order around the compound. Daddy does his best to stay at the houses evenly, but even a single day spent in my house is too often.

I've never been outside of the premises. Never even seen what the rest of the world looks like. One day I will convince Mommy to leave this place with me, but the first and last time I brought it up, she smacked me in the mouth and told me to never say those words again.

I listened, but only because the terror in her eyes scared me into silence.

But I'm even more scared that if I wait any longer, Mommy won't be around long enough to get away from Daddy.

"*Why?*" *I ask on a whisper.*

"*Sibby, honey, don't get sensitive about it. Leonard wanted me to assist with some things in one of the houses, so I did. You were fine here, weren't you?*"

She sits down on a twin bed, directly across from mine. There are over sixty people that attend our Church, so we're all forced to share rooms. I got lucky enough to share a room with Mommy. Though, I know Daddy holds that over my head. It's something he constantly threatens to take away, but never seems to follow through with.

Maybe it's because he knows Mommy is the only one in this Church that has any type of control over me. And Daddy has all the control over her. Like a house of cards, if I fail—so will she.

And I fail a lot.

I think I'm killing my mother.

"*I guess so,*" *I whisper.* "*Daddy didn't hurt you?*"

She sighs, weary and tired. "*Don't ask questions like that, Sibby. Leonard isn't a bad man, he just is doing the best he can for us. He has a lot of responsibility on his shoulders.*"

She lies. She doesn't even believe the words coming out of her own mouth.

Before I can stop it, I curl my lip in revulsion. The only thing he's doing the best he can with is getting people to ride his cock and making my life miserable.

Clearly, he's making her life miserable, too.

Mommy brushes her hair back, thoughtlessly, just to get it out of her eyes. But the small motion turned my life upside down.

Around her neck are deep handprint bruises. She's wearing a turtleneck sweater, which isn't out of the normal for her, especially during winters in Ohio. But her mangy sweater is sagging and exposing the lies Mommy told me.

He did *hurt her.*

Those bruises are not just blue, they're nearly black. *How long and hard do you have to squeeze a woman's throat to turn it that shade?*

My eyes round and a gasp slips from my lips. Her brown eyes snap to mine and they widen ever so slightly. Quickly, she brushes her hair forward again to cover the bruise. But she knew there was no covering up what I had already seen.

Her face falls, and her eyes shift some more.

Mountains of emotions rise to the surface—so many, I fear I'll never be able to climb out of them. Rage. So much rage. Pure, utter heartbreak. Guilt, revenge, sadness. Every emotion a human has ever been plagued by is thrashing in my chest and bleeding into my heart.

I lost some of the red out of my heart in that moment, replaced by a deep, bottomless black. I feel so, so black.

"Why did you lie?" I plead, my lip trembling. A sob climbs up my throat, and there's no stopping the tears. I've never felt like tears were a weakness in front of Mommy. Not when that's all she's ever given me, too.

It's an unspoken understanding. That it's okay to cry in front of one another. But never anyone else.

"Baby..." she trails off, at a loss for words. "It's not your fault, Sibel. You know it's not."

"Then why did he do it?" I snap, enraged by her abuse. By my abuse. By this whole fucking community's abuse. We're all being subjected to it in one form or another, all by the same goddamn man—no. The devil. Fucking Satan himself.

She looks down at her lap, tremors wracking through her nimble fingers. Those same fingers that wiped so many tears away, brushed the hair off my face, helped me up after I had fallen. She was only a child herself when she had me— nowhere close to the maturity she should've been when mothering a child.

She's not perfect, but she's the best mother I could've asked for, given the fragility of her sanity. Her mind is breaking into pieces before my eyes. It has been for eighteen long years, and she's so close to giving up. I can feel it in my bones, and the knowledge sends a fresh dose of panic into my bloodstream. It constricts my lungs like a python, slowly but surely sending me to an early grave.

"Why does he do anything around here?" she whispers under her breath.

70

The words weren't meant for me to hear, but I heard them anyway.

"Let's leave," I say quietly, pleadingly. "Please Mommy. You know he's evil. You know it. We can run away together and start new lives far away from him. Somewhere he'll never find us."

A tear tracks down her cheek. Quickly, she wipes it away like it was never there in the first place.

"I can't," she says, her voice cracking. A sob bursts from her mouth. She slaps a hand over her mouth immediately, quieting the sound.

But you can't silence heartbreak. It's loud and painful. Even after you grieve and heal, it lingers in the background, sliding back into your life just when you think you've overcome it.

Mommy is well-versed in heartbreak; she's been feeling it since the moment she lost her life. Now she's just a shell of a woman, and her soul is ready to find something better.

More tears track down my cheeks. Desperation rises to the surface. Because I don't want Mommy to leave me. I want us to leave here.

I want her to find that something better with me. Together.

Getting up, I rush over to her and sit next to her. The second I cradle her in my arms, she completely loses it. Shattering into tiny pieces in my hands. I want to pick up the pieces, but they're like sand, and slipping through my fingers.

So, I do the only thing I'm capable of right now. Holding her. Comforting her. Loving her.

She lets loose almost two decades worth of trauma, abuse and sadness. She cries so hard, sometimes it takes a full minute for her to regain her breath again. Over and over, until there's nothing left of her to give.

I cry with her, tightening my hold. Feeling her skin on mine. Warm, and soft. I'm desperate to feel her skin, so I hold her hand in my own, while she uses the other to quiet her pain.

Slowly, she regains her composure. Scrambling for her pieces and shoving them back inside her. Still broken, but at least they're not lying at her feet anymore.

Wiping away her tears and then cleaning the snot from her nose with a tissue lying on her nightstand, she straightens back up and clears her throat.

"You shouldn't have had to see that," she says, her voice even but exhausted.

"You shouldn't have gotten punished for my mistakes," I argue.

She shakes her head. "I'm here because of my own mistakes. You're here because of my mistakes, Sibel."

I shake my head, opening my mouth to argue, but she holds up a hand to stop me. A hand that looks like it belongs to an eighty-year old woman, not a twenty-nine-year-old.

"Everything will be okay soon, Sibby. You're stronger than I am. That's why you're the only one that can stand up to Leonard. You have fire in you that I simply do not possess." She pauses and takes a deep breath, as if she's gathering strength for what she's going to say next.

"Which is why you're the only one who can stop him."

My eyes widen as I stare at her with incredulity. She can't be saying what I think she's saying. She gathers herself and leans down into her nightstand. She pulls out a beautiful knife. The handle is a beautiful pink, the wood hand carved and ornate.

It's so... pretty.

I don't know where it came from, or how long she's had it, but it no longer matters. She's giving it to me now. And I'm not sure how to feel about it.

She hands me the knife. When I go take it from her, she resists and looks me deeply in the eyes. "Do you understand what I'm saying?" she asks, placing her other hand on my thigh and squeezing.

Choppily, I nod my head.

"Good girl," she says, patting my thigh and releasing the blade into my hand. "Let's get to bed now."

A strange, overwhelming sensation tugs at me. Without thinking, I wrap Mommy in a hug and hold her tight. In this moment, I know that if I don't, she'll slip through my fingers. She hugs me back just as fiercely, not a single complaint spoken.

"I love you, Mommy," I whisper in her ear.

It takes several swallows before she manages to utter out a, "I love you too, sweet girl. You're going to do great things in life, I just know it."

I leave her alone after that, but I don't take my eyes off her. I lay awake all night, staring at her still form, clutching my new pretty knife in my hand. Hardly blinking, refusing to take my eyes off of her for even a second. She doesn't move from her spot. And that's when she finally slips through.

Early in the morning, when I force my eyes away from her, I look at her alarm and watch it ring out, blaring loud. But she doesn't stir. She doesn't move from her spot at all.

What I didn't know is that before she came to our room, she poisoned herself. I found Ricin left on the bathroom counter after I realized she was dead—she never even tried to hide what she did. The only people who could've gotten that for her are the trusted people who go out every month. When Daddy found out someone betrayed him, he didn't even try to figure out which one got her the poison.

He killed them all.

And I was glad for it. None of those people were pure. And one of them allowed Mommy to leave me here alone. And I hate them for it.

I'll never know the exact moment she took her last breath. I'll never know why she chose to kill herself rather than running away with me.

Or why death was more appealing than a life with me.

But what hurt most is knowing that I spent the entire night staring at my mother's dead body and never even realized it.

Chapter 8

"It's cold here," I complain, whispering low as staff members roam throughout the house, finishing setting up. The big stuff is easy, it's all the small props that become tedious. Picture frames lining the walls, putting fresh linen on the beds. The dozens of mannequins and the rest of the props. I imagine it's tiring.

Good thing Satan's Affair hires a crew in every location to help set up the houses. We're only given a small window of time to settle in the new location and start building before the fair opens. It's fast-paced and can be a little overwhelming with the amount of people that come through.

I always hated waiting for them to put up the walls before I could sneak inside them. I have to wait outside until they're done, keeping away from wandering eyes.

Jackal sits beside me, observing me while I observe the small world outside my walls. Sometimes, I wish I could join them. But it's safer that I stay behind the walls. The less they know about me, the easier my job.

Something tells me they wouldn't be so accepting of me if they knew I'd prefer to lurk behind the walls. That makes people uncomfortable—knowing someone can see you when you can't see them. Personally, I wouldn't mind.

A rush of heat slides through my body when I think about one of my henchmen behind the walls, watching me execute a demon. Watching me paint myself in their blood and then touch myself. Maybe next time, we'll try that.

I love my henchmen. But I get lonely, still. I see friendships like Jennifer's and Sarah's—fake as it was—and feel a bit of jealousy. What would my life be like if I had someone to spend time with? Do girl things with when I want to get away from men.

Would they be accepting of my mission? Possibly even lure them in? It wouldn't hurt to have another woman on the outside, to lure all the evil men in. Not that all evil people are men, but the majority that come through my house happen to be.

I sigh. Jennifer and Sarah are gone now. With Satan's Affair travelling all around the country, they hire a set of people in each location. Cheaper, they say. A lot of the employees return every year, though, providing me with familiar faces. They get paid good money, I've heard, and working at Satan's Affair is an honorable position.

I shiver again, a draft wafting in from the open front door. My costume doesn't provide much warmth, and they're going in and out so often that I can't warm up.

"Want me to warm you up?" Jackal asks. I glance over, seeing him rub his hard dick beneath his trousers. I bite my lip, contemplating.

My men are hard to resist. How could I say no? But... I really should keep an eye on things...

"Guests won't arrive for another twenty minutes," Jackal reminds, seeming to sense that I need convincing. He knows I'm a control freak.

"It's so hard to be quiet though," I argue lightly.

Nothing's happening out there. Nothing important, anyway.

"Get over here, Sibby. Right now."

I squeeze my thighs, my pussy throbbing in response to his sharp command. With a resigned sigh, I pull away from the wall and walk over to Jackal. He stands before I can sit on his lap and signals me to sit on the chair instead.

Just last night, Gary was sitting on this chair, petrified and knowing his life was precariously close to ending. The reminder causes the juncture between my thighs to grow slick.

Ugly as he was, the fear on his face was just so... *cute.*

"Spread your legs," he commands softly, bringing me back to the present.

Tentatively, I open my legs wide for him, baring my pussy. My breath is short, and my cunt throbs beneath his ravenous stare, already anticipating what he's going to do to me. How good he's going to make me feel.

"You have to be quiet," Jackal reminds, dropping to his knees. He swipes his nose through my slit, inhaling as he goes. Fake blood drips from his wide mouth, and the sight reminds me of when I was covered in Gary's blood while he fucked me from behind.

"You smell so good," he groans. I feel a blush creep into my cheeks. A nervous giggle escapes as I shift beneath him. Jackal has always been the most intimidating out of the bunch, even more so than Cronus. Something about the way he walks and talks, the way he carries himself, makes people feel like he's a walking weapon. Quick to strike and capable of killing you in a matter of seconds. I can't lie and say he doesn't intimidate me a little, too.

Hot breath fans across my sensitive flesh, causing goosebumps to rise on my flesh.

"Jackal," I whisper harshly, growing impatient. Yellow eyes peek up at me, a devious smile on his handsome face. Blood spreads across my pussy, but he pays it no mind. We both love it when I'm soaked with blood.

My heart races and I shiver beneath his stare.

I can't help it when he's looking up at me like that—like a God coming home from a bloody, brutal war and finding his wife waiting for him in bed. All my men are handsome, despite the grotesque make up, and Mortis's and Baine's lanky statures. But it's one of the reasons the fair lets them travel along. They draw people in as much as they chase them away.

Like a snake, his tongue slithers out, licking me once before the delicious muscle disappears back into his mouth. I shudder, nearly jumping when his tongue snakes back out again. Right as I open my mouth to berate him again, he closes his mouth over my clit.

My eyes roll, and my mouth opens. It takes strength I didn't know I possessed to keep my moan from bursting out of me. Sensing my turmoil, Jackal narrows his eyes.

"I'll stop if you make a noise," he threatens, the words hummed around my sensitive nerves. I jerk beneath his touch when he flicks out his tongue once more.

Choppily, I nod my head. My straight teeth sink into my bottom lip, trapping it in my mouth and sucking in harshly.

Jackal laps at my cunt slowly, languidly. Happily. As if he's eating an ice cream cone on a hot summer day. Every stroke has my eyes fluttering and my thighs shaking.

When he hits a particularly pleasurable point, a soft moan escapes. His big eyes snap to me, freezing me in place. Again, I bite my lip, hoping he won't stop because of my slipup.

As if conjured out of thin air, Timothy walks in the alcove. When he sees what we're doing, a wide smile stretches across his clown face, showing off his sharp teeth.

"Sibby isn't being quiet," Jackal says, tattling on me. I open my mouth to protest, but Timothy stalks over to me and I'm distracted by the way his muscles move beneath his skin.

"I'll keep her quiet," Timothy answers, his voice low and his smile ominous. My wide eyes watch him prowl towards me, but I lose sight of him when he disappears behind me. When I start to turn, Jackal's mouth latches onto my pussy, sucking in deeply.

I gasp, my head whipping back towards him as a turmoil of pleasure rolls through me. My lids fall, and Timothy is almost forgotten. Until I feel the heat of his presence press in close behind me. His thick cock is hard and pressing between my shoulder blades. He rolls his hips once, enough to show me what I do to him.

Just as another soft moan starts to escape, Timothy's hand snaps to my neck and brings my head flush to his hard stomach. In this position, I can see the entirety of Timothy's clown face as he stares down at me, an excited gleam in his bright blue eyes.

Most would find a clown looking down at them scary, but not Timothy. He's too fucking beautiful to look at.

His hand flexes around my throat, constricting my airways until just a morsel of oxygen is able to leak through.

And with a vengeance, Jackal eats me alive. Biting and licking every inch of my pussy. My chest heaves, and I want to scream from the onslaught, but I can't breathe. I feel my face reddening and my eyes rolling from the mixture of Jackal's sharp tongue and Timothy's unyielding hand.

My stomach tightens as pleasure builds. Stars explode in the back of my eyes as he focuses on my clit—right where I need him. His tongue roves over the bundle of nerves, ecstasy building from the little point his tongue is probing. His hands grab the underside of my thighs and lift, pushing my knees to my chest.

A strangled noise escapes through the vise-like grip on my throat, the new angle wringing out more pleasure. He continues to lick and suck, as his long, textured fingers trail over my opening. The burns on his flesh feel so real, and I love the way it feels inside of me.

I suck in the little breath I can, my legs shaking. Before I can prepare, his fingers are plunging inside me. My mouth opens on a silent scream and my back arches.

I can hardly keep my eyes from rolling, but I do glimpse Timothy's face. He's licking his lips, his gaze hungry and desperate. His other hand trails over my shoulder and down to cup my breast in his large hand. My nipples are nearly cutting holes through my nightgown. He plucks one between his fingers, strumming my nipple and sending shockwaves straight to my pussy.

Another flex of Timothy's hand, warning me to keep quiet. He could sense the groan building in my throat, beneath his hand. Timothy continues to tweak my nipple, squeezing hard until the pain is blinding, and then releasing and allowing Jackal's tongue to steal away the pain.

I can't take it anymore. The coil snaps and my world detonates. Timothy times it perfectly, releasing my throat so the blood releases from my head, causing delirium as I ride the waves. He slaps a hand over my mouth before I can make a peep, though I'm nearly screaming beneath his hand.

I'm breathless as wave after wave of my orgasm rolls through me. I can no longer see, but I can feel my body grinding against Jackal's wide tongue with choppy, desperate movements.

This is the closest I'll ever get to heaven while my soul is trapped in this body.

Slowly, the pleasure fades and when I look down, Jackal is staring up at me with a satisfied smile, my juices covering his burnt face and dripping from his chin.

"Fair is opening soon. Get ready," he orders, his voice strained with hunger.

He stands, prepared to let my juices dry on his face, and walks away, disappearing into the darkness of the hallways.

Following his lead, Timothy walks away, too. But not before turning and winking at me, a victorious smile on his face. I smile in response. Timothy's excitement is always the cutest. He loves seeing me happy and satisfied.

When they're gone, I feel a tad empty again. But I understand. They have to go outside and scare all the guests, chasing them around as they desperately clutch onto their corndogs and cotton candy.

I frown, remembering my muddy cotton candy from yesterday.

That's okay, I'll just steal some more.

Chest still tight, I close my shaky legs and just breathe for a moment. Thinking back, I don't think I made much noise beneath Timothy's hand. Nothing that would've overpowered the banging and loud talking going on outside the walls as the staff finishes setting up.

My house is beginning to quieten, and replacing the loud orders being shouted, is the spooky music that plays on repeat. I've started hearing this music in my sleep now. I've long grown irritated by the sounds, but it's a small price to pay.

Over the next couple hours, loud screeching from outside fills the air. Greasy food begins to waft in, past the smell of plastic and expensive costume makeup.

My stomach growls, and it's as good as time as any to go outside, eat, and scope out the area.

There's no way to be certain that anyone running a pedophile ring would come here. But I understand why Baine thinks they might.

A haunted fair with thousands of children running amuck. Thousands of young girls in revealing clothing, away from their parents and getting into mischief. It's a prime location for someone to snatch up their next victim. With how crowded this fair becomes, it would be nearly impossible to find them once they go missing.

Especially at night, when the monsters come out to play, and groups of friends are scattering like ants and away from each other as they run from their pursuers.

I wait until the coast is clear before crawling out of my hole and hurrying out of the house. An onslaught of shivers consume my body, the chill air harsh against my skin. But when I look up, the shivers fade and my feet slow, my body coming to a stop as I take in the scene before me.

Hordes of people everywhere, laughing and giggling. Eating their weight in food. Screams of laughter as the thrill rides take people hundreds of feet in the air before plunging them back down again. Over and over, in dizzying circles and at a breakneck speed.

When I first started here, I made it a point to steal some tickets and get on every single ride. It was the first and only time I ever rode on roller coasters. It was freeing and exciting, being so high up in the air. Suspended hundreds of feet in the sky, in that small moment in time, was the only time in my life where I felt like Daddy couldn't get me.

I reveled in that feeling the entire night. Especially because I knew it was the last time I'd allow myself that pleasure again.

Like a true believer, I'm devoted to my mission. My time spent on the fairgrounds are restricted to luring demons to my dollhouse and eating—though I'd give that up if my body would allow it.

So, I just watch the guests enjoy the rides. The sound of their thrilled screams and happy laughter always brings me such joy.

Even though it's really cold here in Washington.

Satan's Affair is absolutely incredible. Despite the sun not having completely sunk in the horizon, mosaics of blues, pinks, reds, purples and greens flash in big bulbs alongside every single ride and building in sight. Clouds of colorful smoke drift throughout the night sky from the smoke machines placed throughout the grounds, the colors morphing into new shades from the multicolored lights.

It's just so *pretty*.

Monsters are painted on the food trucks, the scary beings holding up platters of burgers and fries or holding a lemonade. Some of the monsters are depicted as eating the food—elephant ears, hot dogs and deep-fried Oreos posed at their mouths, sharp teeth poking beneath their lips.

My stomach grumbles and I remember myself.

The haunted houses won't open until night falls. So not for another couple hours. The fair doesn't let people in until about five o'clock, allowing them enough time to ride rides and eat before they're drawn into the scary houses.

I skip down the steps and follow my nose to the first food truck I see. They're offering hot fries and philly cheesesteaks. My mouth waters at the smell of salty fried goodness, sizzling meat and a surplus of spices.

The problem with hiding in the walls—I don't get paid for my work. Another small price to pay, but it does force my hand when I need to eat.

A woman walks by with her rowdy young teenagers, pushing a stroller with a sleeping baby inside. I smile, the little cherub's cheeks pink from the chill. The baby is nestled deeply into blankets and a fuzzy jumper. Her long lashes span across her cheeks as she sleeps peacefully, despite the loud screams and chatter surrounding her.

Oh, how I wish to be that innocent and unaware of the depraved world around me again.

"See this little girl, Sibby? She's devoted to God and wants to drink the nectar for herself."

I shake my head harshly, squeezing my eyes shut against the unwanted memories. That twelve-year-old girl birthed some more of Daddy's babies within the next year. She died from complications in childbirth at fifteen years old, her third child—my sibling—a stillborn that dragged its mother's life away with it.

I think that was the nicest thing anyone could have ever done for her. That baby offered her escape, and she took it gladly.

Gritting my teeth, I force myself to focus back on the innocent babe. I would love to go say hi, but babies don't like my face. It's not my fault though, this isn't the type of place for a baby, but I understand some mothers don't have a choice.

I let her walk by, noting the wallet sticking out of her stroller.

I won't steal from a single mother. She looks exhausted already, though a small smile is on her face as she follows her teenagers around, happy because her kids are happy.

A middle-aged man walks by with an angry kid stomping through the grass next to him. The father is yelling at the kid, calling him names as he berates him for running off with his friends. He's a strict father, by the sounds of it. And this kid just wanted to have fun with his friends.

His wallet sticks out of his back pocket as he trudges along, heading towards the exit. His hand is wrapped firmly around the kid's bicep, keeping the kid from running off again. So many times, I remember Daddy holding me the same way. Usually when I ate without praying first and he'd have to force me into the bedroom, keeping me from eating the food.

My siblings would watch on, misery shining in their deadened eyes. They never fought Daddy like I did. They didn't disobey him when his punishment always resulted in scars.

Before my eyes, I see the angry father morph into Daddy, and the kid turns into a younger version of myself. I prance up behind Daddy, light on my feet.

It's too easy. The wallet slips from his back pocket, too focused on embarrassing his poor child. I scamper away, but not before the child spots me. It takes a moment to stop seeing myself—until my red face turns into the little boy's again, brown eyes wide with tears of anger and embarrassment. When he sees my hand, a small smile lifts on his face and he deliberately turns away.

It's entirely possible he might be punished for his father's missing wallet. I can picture it now. A meaty finger pointed in the child's face as he yells with rage, *If you didn't go to that stupid fair, my wallet wouldn't be lost!*

Momentarily, I feel awful. The father's soul isn't rotten and evil, though. He's a strict father, but he loves his kid. That I can tell by the worry etched into the corners of his eyes as he walks away. His soul smells of a bonfire. Smoky, but not rotten.

He just doesn't know how to love the right way. But he'll learn one day, when he pushes his son too far away and learns to regret his actions.

Turning away, I order and pay for my philly cheesesteak with the man's credit card, along with a massive lemonade that my tiny hands have trouble holding onto. I'll toss the card when I'm finished and pocket the cash. There are no cameras in a place like this—no one will be able to trace who exactly used the card. By the time they try, Satan's Affair will be gone.

I park my butt on a bench and watch people pass by as I eat. It's not until I'm sucking down the last of my lemonade that I smell a hint of rot.

Closing my eyes, I lift my chin in the air and try to pinpoint where exactly the smell is coming from. Minutes tick by, and the smell increasingly becomes stronger. Whoever they are, they're coming closer to me.

I open my eyes and focus on each individual. The ones that pass me by, and the ones far off in the background unaware of me. No one escapes my judgment.

A few more minutes go by before the smell of rot is so overwhelming, I nearly upchuck the delicious phillysteak I just ate. The food settles like rocks in my stomach as my gaze desperately seeks out the source of corruption.

There.

An older man, with white hair on the sides of his head and an ugly combover. He's wearing a suit that's tailored to his body perfectly. I would bet fresh cotton candy that his cufflinks are more expensive than his life is worth. Wrapped around his wrist is a gold Rolex. And on that Rolex, barely noticeable, is a small drop of blood.

My eyes narrow into thin slits. He sits down on the bench one over from me. Next to him must be his wife. She looks frail and timid. With freshly dyed red hair, and lipstick to match. Her face is covered in powder, but she didn't bother to extend that make up to hide the bruise on her collarbone.

Maybe she wants others to see. A subtle cry for help.

I turn to blatantly stare at him. My face is blank as I watch the abusive prick sit next to his wife, pointing at random things to attempt to bring a smile to her face. She acquiesces, but the smile is brittle and cracking at the seams. She's dead in the eyes.

Just like her husband will be if I manage to get him inside my house.

Feeling my stare burning into him, he twists his head until his gaze clashes with mine. I suck in a sharp breath, taken aback by the utter emptiness staring back at me. I've come across a lot of evil, rotten souls in my time. Souls I'm certain are burning in the depths of Hell.

But this man... this man's soul was forged *in* Hell. This... *thing* was never human. Not in this lifetime.

A smile cocks on his saggy cheeks. He likes my attention. I may look like a demented, broken little doll, but underneath the makeup is a young girl. I think I'm in my twenties, but with the amount of makeup layered on my face, I could easily pass for sixteen.

Sick, sick man.

I smile at him, showing him my pretty smile. Mortis always says I have the smile of an angel. Demons love angels. They always want what they can never have. They love to taint what's pure. Like picking up a white bunny with hands covered in blood. Angels are used and discarded to the side when they've served their purpose.

Just like Lucifer with Eve. She didn't eat an apple. Lucifer fucked her and ruined her for all men. And then tossed her aside because she could never be Lilith.

The evil man responds in kind, his smile widening so big—even his wife takes notice. She glances at me, her gaze drifting away before snapping back to me, now wide with fear. Her rounded eyes bounce between me and her husband. She's watching her husband prey on another woman, and instead of her burning up with jealously, she fears for me instead.

My dollhouse is only about a hundred feet away—well within sight. I stand up from the bench, offer him a wink and then walk back towards my house. His eyes never waver, I can feel them. Watching me walk into my dollhouse, where he thinks he will find me, drag me off into a dark corner and fuck my innocent little pussy.

How wrong he'll be.

I will be the one to find him. And I will make sure to fuck him just as brutally as the woman he's abused.

Just as I sneak behind the walls, the overhead lights shut off, and the strobe lights turn on. Thick smoke filters out of the machines and slowly builds up in the rooms, filling the room with every color in the rainbow. Phantom fingers curl in the open spaces, masking the monsters hiding within.

It takes another twenty minutes for the doors to open to the public. In that time, as the monsters creep into their hiding spots and wait, there's always a tangy anticipation that settles in the air. The calm before the storm. The silence before the screams.

A group of girls scuttles in first. Hunched together and clasping each other's hands tightly. I inhale deeply and cast my judgement. A garden of flowers greets my nose. I smile, my eyes rolling from the mix of petunias, tulips, and daises.

On cue, the monsters jump out and give chase, forcing them onto the path they're supposed to take.

Familiar screams decorate the poignant air. I shift on my feet, eagerly watching the door. The monsters—a clown with peeling skin and a woman with her chest torn open—get back into their spots and await the next guests.

The front door creaks open, but instead of the sinister older man, it's two beautiful girls. My smile drops and I feel disappointment for a moment before their smell fills the air. Immediately, I'm hit by the smell of jasmine and roses.

My eyes nearly roll, but I keep them focused on the women. Both are beautiful, and stark contrasts to each other. One has long, beautiful cinnamon colored hair, with light freckles dotting her creamy skin. The other has smooth dark brown skin, light green eyes that steal your breath away and a golden hoop in her nose. Both have beautiful bodies, the cinnamon haired girl curvier in the hips, but no less rounded in the right areas than her friend.

I'm not sure what it is about the pair that draws me in. They're magnetic, and I can't help but be pulled into their orbit.

My heart sinks into the pit of my stomach as an odd feeling settles in.

These women are no doubt attracting unwanted attention. It could be from the evil man with the wife, but they could be attracting others, too. What if too many evil souls find themselves in my house, and I can't catch them all?

While my henchmen could overpower several, it would attract attention to *me*. Others wouldn't understand my mission. If I'm caught—I'm done for.

I take a deep breath, watching the pair squeal as the monsters jump out from their hiding spots. They run through the living room, laughing and giggling as they fight to get away.

My stomach churns. I don't know what this feeling is, but I don't like it. It's a foreboding feeling.

Like something bad is going to happen. It's the same feeling I got when I'd say the wrong thing to Daddy or messed up my prayers. His tense silence before he exploded and dragged me off to my punishment.

The monsters go back into position, while my face aches from how hard I'm pressing it into the wall.

The door creaks open, and a shadow casts over the white wooden floors before a large man steps through, a hood pulled over his head. I suck in a sharp breath, my eyes widening at the stature of the man. He's not as big as Cronus, but he's the largest man I've ever seen.

No, it's not his size. It's the way he carries himself.

This isn't just any man.

This is a *dangerous* man.

I inhale, and nearly choke on the scent of him. He doesn't smell rotten, but he smells of fire and brimstone and something... sweet. Like... like burnt roses.

He's definitely not pure. But I can't say he's evil, either. At least not the same type of evil I smelled on the old man earlier.

The man looks left and right, seemingly trying to decide where to go. As he steps in further, the monsters jump out, and he doesn't even flinch. It seems like he doesn't even spare them a glance at all.

He walks into the living room, the monsters still attempting to scare the man.

Eventually, they give up, rolling their eyes and frowning from the odd experience.

Anxiety builds in my chest. He's here for the girls. I just know it.

The door opens again, and rotten egg permeates the air. I choke on the smell and watch as the evil man and his wife step through. Oddly, the demon's eyes snap to the former man's retreating back. His eyes narrow and he licks his lips, heading in that direction as well. The wife yelps when the monsters jump out.

"Quit screaming in my ear," the evil man reprimands sharply. His wife whimpers, but otherwise keeps quiet.

Behind him enters three more men. My eyes widen into saucers, their rotten smells becoming overpowering. The stench makes me gag, along with the now overwhelming anxiety.

Just like I predicted, several evil men are in my house. And I won't be able to kill them all.

And they know each other! I gasp when the old man pauses, his wife stopping alongside him and staring up at him in confusion. He turns to the three demons behind him and inconspicuously nods his head towards the direction that he was walking towards. Is he pointing them towards the large hooded man, or the two girls?

Oh, they are here on a mission. I growl, deep in my chest. No one comes into my house with evil motives and gets away with it.

"There's a doll in here too," the evil man says, talking to the three men trailing behind him. Which means they might be just what Baine warned me of.

These men aren't here to leer and maybe even touch women inappropriately. They're here to *take* them. Steal them away from their homes, never to be seen again.

I bolt, running through the walls and up the stairs. The girls will have to be in my playroom by now, probably about to get chased out by a demented doll hiding under the bed.

I nearly smash my nose into the wall in my haste to find the girls. I release a breath of relief when I see the girls entering the room. They haven't been caught yet. And I need to make sure that doesn't happen.

All five men must be together. They came in one after the other, all following after the girls. For the life of me, I can't fathom why five men preying on two girls would be necessary.

Doesn't matter. They're all sick, sick people. And even if I can catch one of them, that'll be better than nothing.

The doll crawls out from under the bed, chasing after the girls. She took over Jennifer's job, but she's not nearly as skilled at it.

I bite my lip, and growl with frustration. I'm not *crazy*, there's no way I'll be able to trap five men and take them down all at once! Not during operation hours. Who do I choose?

I grab my hair and pull as indecision claws at me. The hooded man scares me most. He's lacking the rotten smell but he's definitely the most dangerous. And he'll look the cutest tied up in my chair, bleeding beneath my pretty pink blade. Maybe if I'm lucky, I can catch the old man with the wife, too—if only it means freeing that poor woman from her abuser's clutches.

I need to catch the hooded man before he enters this room. I won't be able to trap him with another person in the room to witness it. The doll shuts the doors again and crawls back under the bed, awaiting the next guest. I run towards the hallway outside of the playroom, where Jackal stands at the end.

The hooded man comes into view, and immediately I start singing from inside the walls. The man freezes, his body completely immobile as I continue to sing my haunting lullaby.

At the end of the hallway, Jackal comes to life. His head turns towards the man. I can't see the man's eyes, but it seems as if he spots Jackal. To my surprise, he heads straight towards my henchman. My singing ceases, surprised by the nerve. Most stay away from Jackal. He's stationed at the end of the hallway to deter people from going down that direction. Their path is supposed to go through my playroom first.

The man brushes past Jackal and enters into another bedroom. Seeing my opportunity, I take a risk and scramble out of the small door and into the hallway.

I run towards Jackal, whose head is now turned back towards me with a quizzical expression. He's surprised too.

"We need to get him *now*," I rush out. Jackal follows me into the room. I stop short when I see the large man standing in the middle of the room, his back facing me as he looks around. We're in another playroom filled with mechanical monsters. One bursts from the pink armoire in the far corner of the room. Another bursts from a closet filled with baby girl clothing.

Slowly, the man turns towards me. His face is still hidden. The flashing strobe lights do little to provide me with enough light to see his face. I just make out his lips and chin.

"Where are they?" he asks. I shiver from the sound. His voice is deep, but what makes my spine tremble is the smokiness to his tenor.

His voice emulates his scent. Fire and brimstone.

"Safe from you," I say, as Jackal walks around me and comes to stand beside me. The man doesn't pay my henchman any attention. I frown. That angers me. He doesn't appear the least bit intimidated and I don't like it.

I look at Jackal. "Let the others know two women are being followed and make sure they get away safely. I have this handled."

Jackal nods, trusting me to handle this man and leaves.

I managed to capture one, but the other four men will still be stalking the girls. They're not safe yet.

A small smirk is on the man's face.

"So you're crazy, huh?" he asks quietly.

I rear back, shocked by his assumption. I am *not* crazy.

"Don't call me that," I snap. "You're the one preying on women."

He cocks a brow. "That just makes me disturbed. Not crazy."

Anger fills my lungs, like a flood bursting through a dam. I clench my fists, my nails biting into my skin. Red crescent moons imprint in the flesh of my hand. This man is... I can't wait to kill him.

I slide my pretty knife out from under my nightgown. I always have it strapped to my thigh for quick access. I can't see them, but I know he's eyeing the blade, the dull metal glinting under the strobe lights. I kick my foot back, catching the door and shutting it firmly behind me.

I'm not entirely sure he'll fit in the walls. But maybe if I can chop his arms off really quick, he'll fit.

"What are you going to do with that, dolly?" he mocks, a sinister smile widening his lips. My eyes thin, and I nearly choke on the rage.

How dare he! This is *my* dollhouse, and he has the audacity to disrespect me like this.

"I'm going to kill you, monster.

Chapter 9

Silence greets me.

"Why would you do that?" he questions after a pregnant pause, taking a threatening step towards me.

For one single second, I lapse into a moment of insanity and almost take a step back. His image flickers, and for a split second, I see Daddy looming before me. I focus on the man and steel my spine, forcing myself to hold my place.

This monster will *not* intimidate me in my own home. Especially when *I'm* not the one that should be scared.

"Because I've cast my judgement," I say, my own smile ticking up the corners of my mouth. "And you've failed. You're an evil man, and you were here to hurt two women."

"Two?" he queries, feigning stupidity.

"Yes," I growl. "You deserve to die for what you had planned."

"And what did I have planned?" He takes another step towards me. White hot rage prickles at my flesh. I do him the same honor and take one towards him.

He pauses, just for half a second, before he recovers and smiles. It was enough. He was surprised.

I giggle, an evil smile ticking at the corner of my lips. "Don't play stupid, demon. You were going to kidnap them. Probably rape and torture them. You would've let your goons do the same. And then either kill them or sell them off to someone."

He doesn't speak. He just stares at me, his chest rising and falling in a steady, calm rhythm.

"Is that what you think?" he challenges, his voice deeper and huskier. He's angry.

"That's what I know," I sass.

"Then it seems we're done here," he concludes before briskly walking towards me. I'm not sure if his intentions are to leave or to hurt me, but I don't wait to find out. I charge at him, swiping my blade across his face.

But I miss. He bends backwards, the tip of my blade several inches from his face. It happens in almost slow motion—when he bends backwards and I catch the first glimpse of his face. I gasp, surprised by the sight.

And then time speeds. Like a viper, his hand snaps out and catches my wrist. I kick my leg out, my foot kicking in his kneecap. He stumbles, his hand dropping my wrist in surprise.

I bring my knife down in an arc, but he swivels out of the way.

"Feisty bitch," he mutters, an almost amused pitch to his tone.

Growling, I continue to swipe my knife at him, backing him further into the room. I need to hurry and knock him out before someone stumbles in. My men will keep guests away as much as they can, but that doesn't mean other staff members won't take notice to discord in the system.

The man dodges each strike, seamlessly and swiftly. It looks as if he's dancing and the fact that I don't look as graceful as he does angers me further. He looks like something out of a film, the way his body curves around my knife, the strobe lights making him look like he's skipping through time and space. It's clear this isn't the first time this man has been in a knife fight.

Of course it isn't. He's a fucking kidnapper! An evil, twisted demon who steals the innocent and auctions them off just to get money in their pockets. All for money and power.

It sickens me.

He has to die. And he'll look so cute strung up by his entrails tonight, with his blood painting my body in red. I'll dance on his shredded body, and let my henchmen play with me, too.

Growing frustrated, I grip my pretty knife and launch it at him. I didn't expect it to strike true, but to cause enough distraction to wrestle him down.

He's much bigger and stronger, but that can be limiting. I'm smaller and can slip out of positions easier than he can.

Problem is, he doesn't fall for my trick. The prick leans to the side, the knife whistling past his head and lodging into the wall. A normal person would look back at the knife, surprised by the move. But not him. He just continues to glare at me beneath his hood.

The hood has fallen back far enough in our fight that I can now see the entirety of his face. Electrifying mismatched eyes stare back at me, rimmed by long, thick lashes. One eye so dark, it looks black. And the other an ice blue so light, it looks white. Yin and yang.

A thin, white raised scar cuts down through his left eye, giving his face a brutally masculine look.

That face is mesmerizing. It's dangerous.

"I've been trying not to hurt you," he growls, low in his chest. The sound of imminent danger in his tone forms a pit in my stomach. I never fear the demons, but this one has my heart racing and palms slick with sweat.

Which is exactly why he needs to die.

"Pity. I've been trying to do the exact opposite," I snap.

A small smile graces his lips. In another life, he'd fit right in with my henchmen.

He's beautiful and terrifying all in the same breath, inhaling terror and exhaling a haunting beauty. It *hurts* to look at him. His face is scarred, his eyes are unsettling. A hard life lingers on the edges of his mouth. His beauty can only be seen on the face of the Devil. Tempting, but would eviscerate you in a matter of seconds.

"Your soul is made of brimstone and fire," I whisper, stepping closer to him. "Come to me, little demon. I'll show you what the devil really looks like."

His smile widens and he meets me halfway, blocking every one of my strikes with ease, but not managing to make any hits of his own, either. We're nearly evenly matched.

I've been fighting my entire life. Fighting Daddy and his punishments. Fighting to get out of a dangerous cult, just to fight the demons that riddle this Earth with filth. I'm no stranger to using my hands to defend myself no less than I use them to kill.

I manage to land a fist across his cheek. He doesn't flinch from the impact but absorbs it like the towels Timothy uses to clean up demon blood.

He looks at me, his eye twitching with anger. He pauses, and despite my brain screaming at my body to keep fighting, my limbs freeze as well. And just like before, his hand whips out, striking like a viper and crunching straight into my nose.

My head snaps back as sharp pain explodes across my face. Stars dot my vision, and the force of his punch sends me stumbling backwards. My slippers lose their traction, and I'm falling backwards.

Blood spurts from my nose and I let loose a frustrated squeal.

The fucking audacity! The nerve of this lowly parasite!

I glare at him and bare my bloody teeth.

"I will fucking kill you," I threaten. I spit out a mouthful, not enjoying the taste of my own blood any more than the blood of monsters.

"Yeah, you said that," he mutters, before storming past me, whipping open the door and storming into the hallway.

I scramble upwards, expecting to see Jackal hauling him back into the room. But that doesn't happen. I hear a grunt, and by the time I'm skidding out into the dark hallway, Jackal is flat on his back.

"Jackal!" I screech, stomping my foot. Squeals of laughter filters through, and I slinker back into the room before someone catches me. I breathe in deep—through my mouth—and breathe out. My nose is throbbing and clogged with blood. Blood that is still painting my face and dress in rivulets of crimson. No one would look twice at me in a setting like this, but I don't want my face to be seen.

Gently, I prod my nose, finding that it's completely broken.

No matter. Daddy has broken my nose a few dozen times.

"You act like a demon, I'll make you look like one, too, Sibel."

I take a deep breath, position my hands and snap the bone back into place. I squeeze my eyes shut tightly, willing the tears to go back down. It doesn't matter that I've felt that pain before, it still really fucking hurts.

I stomp my foot again, this time to release some of the pent-up anger swirling like a Cat 5 hurricane in my chest cavity. Filling it as steadily as the blood filled my dress.

I'm going to slice this revolting parasite open, piece by piece until he's chopped into a million different pieces.

Crawling back into the wall, I storm through the hallways, checking the rooms to see where my prey has run off to. I stop short when I see the man in the same room as the four older men and the wife.

A smile grows on my face, and excitement drums in my pulse, quickly replacing the anger. I squeal, not caring if they hear me, and run towards the door. I hear the man I had just attacked groan in what sounds like frustration. He must've heard my delight and sensed me coming.

Just as I thought, when I quickly crawl into the room, the man is already staring at me. Frustration and anger are evident on his scarred face.

"For the love of God, please leave me alone," he says.

"God has nothing to do with this, silly," I chirp, giggling at his evident anger at seeing me again. What did he think I'd do, just let him go? How *cute*.

The four older men all turn towards me, shock splayed across their faces. One of them remembers himself and smooths his face into what should look welcoming. He has white hair like the rest of them but wields sharp baby blue eyes. If I dissected those eyes, I'm sure I'd find that they have seen all kinds of sick and depraved things. Things done by his own two hands, sporting an evil smile on his wrinkled face.

He lifts his hands in a placating gesture. "Hey there, we're incredibly sorry to linger. We were just talking. We'll get out of your way so the other guests can come through."

"I'd rather you stay," I answer. My eyes clash with the wife's, her green eyes round with fear. I try to convey that everything is going to be okay in a single look, but I think she's too far in the depths of hysteria. I'm a bloody mess, and I don't know what the scarred man was saying to these men, but it has the woman shaken.

It's physically impossible for me to take on all of these men at once. Especially if the scarred man is here, too. I barely held my own against him, and in the end, he got away.

I'll definitely have to bring in reinforcements. I just don't know how to do this without attracting unwanted attention.

Huffing, the scarred man charges towards me. I raise my hands in a defensive move, but he smacks them away, wraps his calloused hand around my throat and slams me into the wall. Before I can lodge my knee deeply into his balls, he leans down and speaks lowly in my ear.

"Listen to me and listen to me carefully. We have a common enemy here. Those four men are extremely dangerous and sick men. You're vastly outnumbered, and while I can take on four decrepit men, you would make my life easier if you'd help. So, let's set our differences aside for the time being, kill these assholes together, and then you can try and fail to murder me after? Deal?"

My mouth slackens, shocked by his proposition.

Never, *never*, did I think this would happen.

A throat clears from in front of me. I peek over the man's shoulder to see the four men starting to drift towards the door. The husband has his wife's bicep firmly clasped in his arm and is starting to drag her towards the door.

Just like Daddy.

Making a split decision, I grit out, "Fine. We'll knock them out. I can get them inside the walls and keep them there until the fair shuts down. But I promise you this,

I will *not* fail when we've finished. And I *will* kill you."

He doesn't acknowledge me. Instead, he steps away and charges towards the first man within reach. They scatter like cockroaches, all skittering towards the two doors.

If I had my henchmen with me, this would be over far quicker. But a large part of me is very curious about the scarred man that broke my nose, and so I keep my henchmen away for now.

I run after the man closest to me. He doesn't even see me coming, too intent on getting away. I grab his jacket and press my fingers into his pressure point.

He drops, and I move on to the husband.

"Not so fast, asshole," I snap, grabbing him by the back of his suit jacket. His wife screams, startled as her husband is jerked away from her. He grips her arm harder as I haul him backwards, causing her to stumble and fall on her knees.

I gasp, appalled by what he just did.

"That was *not* nice!" I bellow, slapping the man across the face. The husband fights me, but my finger is pressing into his pressure point and he's dropping like a sack of potatoes within seconds.

When he drops, the wife's screams die, but the fear has her scrambling away.

"Hey!" I shout, right before her hand clasps the doorknob. She pauses, and looks over her shoulder at me. She's trembling, and I'm concerned she'll go into shock soon.

"You won't have to worry about him anymore, okay?" I say, pointing towards her unconscious husband. Her eyes follow my finger. She looks at her husband with a mixture of fear and relief. A battle wages in her eyes. To save him or leave him. But we both know what she'll decide. If she leaves, she's free. *Free.* I'll never forget my first taste of it, and I'm very sad I won't get to witness hers.

"What are you going to do?" she asks finally, her voice trembling.

"Don't you worry about that. Just rest assured, you will never see him again. And you can live in peace now. But if you tell anyone about this and what happened, I'm afraid I will have to fix that. Don't make me regret letting you go."

I don't kill innocent people. But in this case, letting her go is a gamble.

Her green eyes hold mine for all of two seconds before she's muttering out a, "I promise," and scrambling out of the door before I can change my mind.

"You do realize that was stupid, right?" a deep voice says from behind me. I nearly jump, twirling to see the scarred man standing before the four unconscious men.

"Would you have killed her?" I challenge.

He doesn't hesitate. "No. But I certainly wouldn't have let her run free, either."

Before I can ask what the hell that even means, he's leaning down and picking up one of the men by the collar of his shirt and dragging him towards my crawlspace door.

"Let's hurry up, please," he grits through clenched teeth.

I let it go for now, and hurry through the door and drag the man in. One by one, he drags the men over, and I slide them into the hallway.

"I got it from here. The fair closes at eleven o'clock. It'll take the staff about forty-five minutes to clear out so meet me back here at midnight," I instruct. Just before I close the door, I remember myself and open it back up. He's halfway through the exit door when I stop him.

"Hey!" He turns to me. "What's your name?" I ask.

He considers me for a moment, but ultimately shakes his head, and says, "Zade."

"You're not going to hurt those girls, are you, Zade?"

When he just stares, I clarify. "The girl with light brown hair, and the pretty black girl. You'll leave them alone, right? Because if you don't, our deal is off and I'm killing you first."

A small smirk tugs on his lips. He really is an incredible-looking man.

"They'll be in good hands. Scouts honor," he says, saluting me with a smartass look on his face. I scowl, not knowing what that means but sure of the fact that he's mocking me.

Thinning my eyes, I suss him out. Daddy used to tell family members of his follows the same thing. And he was always lying when he said it.

"Don't worry, your mother is in very good hands. Here, she will be able to follow the path the Lord has set for her."

So, that can mean a lot of different things, and some of those things could very well be evil intentions. He doesn't give me time to come to a conclusion. He turns and shuts the door behind him.

What a strange, strange man.

Deciding that I can't save them all, despite those two women's otherworldly scents, I focus on the matter at hand. I have four, saggy men unconscious in my hallway. I don't know how exactly the scarred man knocked the other two out, but I know my two aren't going to be out for too much longer. I could paralyze them with pressure points, but I usually don't prefer that method.

Takes the fun out of it for me. And I *really* like having fun.

I hurry through the hallways and locate Cronus and Baine. With quick urgency, I get them to help me drag the men by the stairs and tie them up. Problem is, I only have one chair here.

I've never had more than one demon at a time. So, I'm left with the only option. I locate their pressure point near the spinal cord and press hard until there's no chance of them getting up anytime soon. There's no way to know for sure if it's permanent, but no matter. I'll have Mortis keep watch over them and make sure they don't escape.

Learning pressure points is the only thing I can thank Daddy for. He had a weird fascination with being able to debilitate or even kill someone with a single jab of his finger. All that power to ruin or end someone's life in one small movement.

I begged him to teach me, and despite the fact that I loathed Daddy, I spent hours with him for over a year until I learned every single point in a human's body.

I'm unstoppable. And when the scarred man and I are done killing off the demons, I will turn to him and serve him the same fate.

I've already cast my judgement. And once I've made my decision, no one can stop me from carrying out my duty.

Chapter 10

"What took you so long?" I snap, letting the man with mismatched eyes back into my empty dollhouse. I'm angry. He's thirty minutes late and this bastard of a man is wasting my time! The four demons have been awake for the past half hour and wreaking havoc on my sanity with their loud pleas and escape attempts.

I've never had this many at once and I've already nearly yanked all my hair from my head.

Zade walks further into the room, staring behind me. My henchmen stand behind me, crowding the foyer of the house. Their colored eyes pick apart Zade, eyeing him like hungry dogs. They know my plans later. They know they'll get their turn.

The scarred man casts his eyes over my henchmen, and then sweeps the area as if he's looking for other people hiding in the house. Ultimately, he doesn't give my henchmen further thought. He mistakenly is deeming them non-threats, but he will learn the hard way that they're anything but.

"I got caught up with something," he murmurs. In one quick sweep, I notice that his lips are puffy, with a tiny droplet of blood on his bottom lip, as if someone bit him. His black hair is mussed, looking like hands pulled at his hair, and the collar of his shirt beneath his hoodie is stretched out.

If I didn't know any better, he looks like he just engaged in a very intense make-out session. I scowl, miffed that he made me wait just so he could smack lips with some girl.

So fucking rude. I can't wait to kill him later.

"Where are they?" he queries, bringing my attention back to his face.

I notch my head up, indicating towards the stairs. "In my playroom."

He quirks a brow but keeps silent as I lead him towards the stairs.

"Stay down here until I call you guys up," I order my henchmen.

"Sibby, are you sure? I don't trust this guy," Mortis asks, stepping forward and eyeing the scarred man with disdain.

Zade is staring at my men, his brow lowered with an expression I can't quite place. I don't know if he's offended by not being trustworthy or what, but he doesn't look amused.

"I can handle myself," I reply before continuing up the stairs.

Zade follows suit and clears his throat. "So, what's your deal?" he asks quietly.

His voice is deep and sounds like gravel is encrusted around his voice box. Gritty, and smoky. A very alluring voice, I must admit.

"What do you mean, *my deal*?" I reiterate sharply. He makes it sound as if I'm diseased.

"Those people you were talking to—do they not like me?" he asks, amusement coloring the deep timbre of his voice.

"My henchmen? No. Nor do they trust you."

"You uh, told them to stay down there and that you can handle yourself?" he continues. "They're not coming up too?"

I pause on the steps, forcing him to come to a stop as well. We haven't even made it up the stairs and he's already grinding my nerves. Not that he cares, by the looks of it. I look back at him with my brow lowered. "Do you see them behind you?" I wave my hand behind him.

He doesn't turn to look. He just smirks. "No."

"Then there's your answer! I don't need my henchmen to protect me from *you.* And since you're here, I figured they could sit this one out," I explain impatiently, my irritation spiking.

He's silent for a beat and then, "Ah."

"*Ah*?" I repeat, aghast. "What does that mean?"

"It means you're fucking insane, little girl. Where are these demons again, or whatever you call them?"

I already told the idiot where they are, but whatever. I huff and lead him into my playroom, curling my fists tight just to keep them from smashing his stupid face in.

Inside are the four men strapped to chairs. After the staff left for the night, Jackal went and found three other chairs so I didn't have to deal with anyone escaping. Though I did paralyze three of them, two of them only experienced it briefly and were able to move again. The other was complaining about not being able to feel his legs until I broke each and every one of their ankles. He shut up after that.

As soon as the demons see us, they immediately start screaming into the duct tape covering their mouths and wriggling like little bugs in their seats.

"Do they know you?" I ask.

Zade hums in confirmation, looking over their broken ankles and sweaty, red faces. I lit up this room with extra lighting and took out the strobe lights. Something told me Zade would've kicked the strobe lights in just to get them to stop and I didn't want to worry about replacing them for tomorrow when the fair reopens.

"You sure no one can hear them?" Zade asks, glancing around the room.

"I do this all the time."

With that, he side-eyes me.

"You kill people often?"

105

I shrug. "Only the demons."

I don't care about divulging information to this man. He's going to die anyways. What does it matter if I tell him I kill demons all the time?

His lip quirks up, and there's a derisive gleam in his eye. "Do you call yourself the demon-slayer too?"

Rage nearly slaps me in the face at his disrespectful tone. I stomp my foot and screech, "You're not funny!"

He cocks a brow at my outburst, but that glint in his eye doesn't dissipate. My lip curls. I can't wait to stab my pretty knife through his eyes. They will not be mocking me when he sees the pointed end coming straight towards them, will they?

I turn my attention back to the four men as potent fury rattles my bones. For now, I'll take it out on the wriggling parasites before me. *Then*, I'll rip Zade's eyes from their sockets before I kill him.

Zade pays me no mind and walks towards the man that came to Satan's Affair with his wife. He crouches down until he's eye level and slowly observes the struggling man.

"I've been watching you for quite a while, Mark," he says lowly. Almost impossibly, his voice deepens even further. "Do you know why?"

Mark frantically shakes his head, staring at Zade like a friend that betrayed him.

The man, Mark, shouts something but the duct tape prevents his words from being clear. Zade rips the tape from the man's mouth, leaving a red welt in its wake. The old man grunts from the pain.

"Zack, I don't understand what's going on. Whatever is wrong, please don't do this. We were friends!"

Zack? Why is he calling him Zack?

"My name isn't Zack. Call me Z."

At the mention of his nickname, Mark's eyes widen almost comically. Like one of those anime characters with eyes too big for their faces.

"Z? Y-you're Z? *The* Z?"

I roll my eyes, sighing dramatically. Zade looks like he kills people often, but I don't see what's so scary about him.

No matter, Z obviously has some type of reputation and whatever it is has Mark vibrating in his chair from fear, as if an earthquake is tearing through his insides.

"The very one, Mark."

"Look, Z, I don't know what you think I did but you have it all wrong."

"Do I?" Zade queries, his dry tone bored.

"You do! Look. This is about that leaked video, isn't it? I don't know anything about that, I swear! My partner was the one in that video."

At the mention of his partner, another old man comes to life—the one with numb legs. Muffled screams vibrate the tape on his mouth, and he fights his binds with renewed energy. He has random tufts of white hair on his bald head and is glaring at Mark with the heat of a supernova.

"Really, Mark, you're going to blame your sadistic ritual all on Jack? How unoriginal. Your face can be seen clear as day, dickhead."

I sigh, growing bored of this conversation.

"Yes, we knew these men were evil and exploiting innocent girls. Let's get a move on with the killing, *Z*," I whine.

Zade looks over his shoulder at me and gives me a *what are you waiting for* look.

"By all means, start the killing," he says, waving his hand towards the other three men. "Don't let me stop your demon-slaying."

I *almost* throw my knife at him. The worst part is the asshole keeps his back to me, meaning he doesn't feel threatened by me.

Big mistake.

Very big mistake.

Deciding I no longer care, my anger gets the best of me. I whip my knife straight towards the back of his head. With cat-like instincts, Zade swerves and the knife lodges into Mark's stomach instead. A loud, garbled yell bursts from the man's throat. Bright red blood sprouts from the wound.

Slowly, Zade turns his head to look at me. Instinctively, I swallow and take a small step back. His face is a blank mask, but something dark and animalistic is glittering in the depths of his eyes. It's the most chilling look I've ever seen and ices my bones from the marrow out.

I've never seen anyone dodge a knife without even seeing it was coming. Or *where* it was coming from.

"You good, demon-slayer?" he asks, cocking his brow. I want to stab something every time he gives me that stupid look. I hate how intimidating the action is. The way his eyebrow arches is as undeniably alluring as it is threatening.

"Stop mocking me," I spit. As much as this man likes to look scary, I'm confident he can't hurt me.

"Consider it a pet name," he says off-handedly before turning back around.

Huffing, I stomp towards one of other men that hasn't been identified yet. I don't care what his name is. Just that he bleeds.

I plant my foot in his chest and kick back. A muffled outburst sounds through the tape as he knocks straight back. With his arms tied behind the back of the chair, he lands right on his wrists. He screams. Must've broken his wrists.

Oopsies.

White hot rage still clouds my vision as I straddle his body and plunge my knife into his chest and neck. The other men start screaming as they witness their friend's brutal death.

"Jesus," Zade mutters from behind me.

I don't *care*. He's always making fun of me, always looking at me like I'm crazy!

"Don't you dare look at me like that, Sibel. You look crazy, and God doesn't accept crazy people into his Kingdom."

"I'll show you a demon slayer," I mutter breathlessly through more stabs.

Blood splatters across the entire front of my body. My face, my hair, all over my already ruined dress. The man's eyes roll to the back of his head as he suffocates on his own blood.

"Think you got him," Zade announces from behind me, sounding a little annoyed.

I *still* don't care. I keep stabbing. The knife elicits wet, slurping noises. I change my trajectory and start stabbing him in the face. At one point, his eyeball lodges onto the tip of my knife and pops out of the socket.

At that point, Mark turns to the side and starts upchucking.

I barely register the sigh that blows past Zade's lips, nor the calm footsteps as he walks over to me and grabs my wrist midair.

I whip towards him, seething mad.

"Now you're going to stop me from demon slaying?!" I shriek, my voice pitching to near hysteria.

"Little girl, there's quite a few things you need to get serious help for, but I'd say anger management is top of the list."

My eye twitches as the anger circulates.

Sometimes I get like this. The littlest things set me off, and I can't control the pure rage flowing through my body. Mommy always said I need to stay cool—to not let people see how much they're getting to me. But I never could, no matter how much I tried.

His grip on my bloody wrist tightens when I try to yank it from his grasp.

"Look at me," he demands. I comply immediately, my wide eyes snapping towards him. His unique face starts to blur. "Drop the knife," he orders next. This time, I try to fight the pull to listen to him. I'm *not* submissive. But something about this man makes me want to be.

"What's your name?" he asks quietly.

I huff like an enraged bull with a red flag being waved in my face.

"Sibel." Casting my eyes down, I lick my dry lips and hesitate. I glance up at him and awkwardly say, "My friends call me Sibby."

His eyes trace my face. He looks like he's trying to figure something out, and I'm not sure if I appreciate it. I feel the blood rushing to my face as his eyes pick me apart.

"You're an interesting person, Sibby. But I'm going to need you to calm the fuck down. I can't interrogate in peace when you're over there stabbing someone like a cracked-out banshee, you feel me?"

Normally, being told to calm down would heighten my anger, but the fact that he deliberately used my nickname—that he considers me a *friend*—is what ultimately calms my nerves. My henchmen are all I have. I don't think I've ever had a real friend before.

Especially not one that doesn't cower from my calling in life.

I swallow thickly and reluctantly nod my head. "Are you done mocking me?" I ask, my voice more timorous than I'd prefer. I don't know why, but something about Zade just makes me want to listen. Makes me want to seek guidance from him. Maybe it's because I never had a real father, and Zade asserts a platonic dominance over me that I always sought from Daddy, but never found.

He smirks. "I think I've taken a liking to my nickname for you. But I'm no longer making fun when I say it," he placates.

I eye him closely, reluctant to believe it. He's granting me his own special nickname? My heart jumps in my chest, and it feels something like giddiness.

He doesn't bother trying to convince me. He drops my wrist, plucks the knife from my hand and drags the tip on the floor until the eyeball pops off.

More gagging follows suit from the demons, while I watch him mechanically. No one touches my pretty knife.

No one.

He wipes the blood off on his black jeans and then hands it back to me.

My fingers slowly curl around the knife as I eye him, an odd look on my face. I have no idea what I'm supposed to be feeling right now.

He winks at me and then walks back over to Mark.

I take the opportunity to pick through the teeth. I smile triumphantly when I see black eroding this man's teeth. The sign of decay.

"Mark, are you going to give me the information I need? I want to know where you do the rituals," Zade demands, his voice devoid of emotion once more.

"Z, I *swear*, I don't know anything!" Mark wails, vomit trailing from his thin lips.

Calmly, Zade picks up his hand, digs the tip of his own blade under his fingernail and pops it off with a quick flick of his wrist.

The man screams, his face turning an alarming shade of red and purple.

"Try again," Zade says evenly. He positions the tip of the knife under another nail, readying for another lie.

"Z, I'm not lying to you!" Another nail, followed by more wails of agony. Once again, Zade positions the knife under the next nail. He slowly lifts the nail, giving the demon plenty of time to cut in.

He takes the bait.

"Okay, wait, wait! S-some of the people we take, we take them to an underground club. Their blood gives us power unlike anything you've ever seen."

My eyes widen, and without realizing it, I've dragged myself off of the dead man and wandered close to the pair. Zade shoots me a warning glare to stay back, but otherwise doesn't mind my presence.

"Where is this place?" Zade asks.

"You can only access it through a private Gentlemen's club—*Savior's*. You need special access to even get in the club, let alone gain access to the..." he trails off, his face tightening as if he's dreading his next words. He takes in a deep breath, and something like acceptance settles in his eyes. "To gain access to the dungeon."

Dungeon? What the hell kind of demons are these people?

"Yeah? And what do you do in this dungeon?"

Clearly, Zade knows exactly what they do, but it seems like he wants verbal confirmation. Like he wants this man to admit to his sins. Makes his death a little more justifiable.

Mark doesn't like that question. His eyes shift nervously and his mouth flops, but no sounds come out. With another flick of his wrist, Zade tears off another nail.

I smile, giddiness at this man's suffering bubbling to the surface. It is so pleasing to see them cry and beg for their lives.

Pleas that will go as unanswered as their pleas to the fake gods they claim to worship.

"Fuck, Z! I-I just..." he trails over, as sweat profusely pours into his eyes. He blinks against the sting, more tears trailing down his ruddy cheeks. A sob breaks loose, and Zade positions his knife under the next nail.

"Wait! I said, wait, goddammit! We uh—we perform rituals on them." He squeezes his eyes shut as soon as the admission leaves his chapped lips.

My mouth pops open as Zade growls out, "Why?"

Mark tightens his lips, a pained expression on his red face. "That's how we're sworn into the secret society. We must perform a ritual and mark ourselves as children of the Eternal Rebirth. They are cosmic entities and the true authority over this world."

A plethora of emotions filter through my bloodstream. Rage. So much fucking rage. Disgust, sadness, and even a stab of sharp pain when I think about the pain those poor children are suffering through. All to join a fucking *society?*

"And this society, you traffick children? Sell them, rape, torture and kill them?"

A single nod, guilt shining in his eyes. Not guilt over what he's done to innocent souls, but only because he got caught and is now suffering the consequences.

"Is that all you do?"

"No, but that's the only thing we do that you have a chance of putting a stop to—as small as it is. The rest is deep operations within the government, a lot of it specifically to keep control over the people and make them think they have any control over what happens in their lives."

He glances at me, and an unreadable expression morphs his face. Now... now he truly looks like a demon. He looks flat-out sinister.

"If I were you, I wouldn't bother saving them. I would focus on saving yourselves first."

I step towards him, readying my knife to plunge into whatever body part I reach first, but Zade stops me. His hand swings out, and he casts me a warning look over his shoulder.

But I can see it in his eyes, too. The rage glittering in his yin-yang pools. The desire to torture this man until he's pleading for death.

"All of you? You all have done this ritual?" Zade asks after a beat, directing his question towards the other two men. He ignores Mark's ominous warning, but all I want to do is ask what the hell he even means by that.

The other men are all sweating, their white hair molded to their heads, and with potbellies and sagging chins. They all look the same, with slight differences. Old men that have so much money, they've grown bored with life. There's nothing that excites them anymore.

Nothing, except little helpless girls and boys, and their cries of pain.

"If you lie, your death will be slow. My demon slayer and I have plenty of ideas on how to make it the most painful last hours of your miserable life." I shiver from his words. From the deep timber in which he speaks and how he claimed me as *his*.

I smile big. I have my first friend.

I hope he gets along with my henchmen. I'm sure once they get over their initial suspicions, they'll accept him into our little group. As a brother, and as a friend. Just like I'm already starting to.

I'm snapped out of my musings at another muffled yelp. Jack tried denying the question anyway, and Zade answered that by stabbing the knife deep into his thigh.

"That's just a taste, Jack. Brad, how 'bout you? You like to fuck children, too?" Brad, the man with bright blue eyes that spoke to me earlier, nods his head like a child with a marker in his hand standing next to the drawings on the wall.

Pathetic. Disgusting waste of human flesh and organs.

I bounce on my feet, restlessness taking over.

"Can I play now, Zade?" I ask impatiently.

He straightens and nods towards Jack and Brad. "Go ahead and have fun with those two. I have a couple more things to get out of dear old Mark first."

"If you don't let me go, I won't tell you anything else! Nothing!" Mark shouts. The bargain is weak. Mark knew from the beginning he was never walking out of this haunted dollhouse. He's just not willing to accept his fate yet.

"You're a weak man, Mark. You'll tell me anything I want to know once the pain becomes too much. You either die slow, or quick."

I tune out Mark's desperate pleas and arguments and turn my attention to the monsters before me. When they sense my stare, and the absolute pleasure already radiating throughout my body, they start fighting their bonds.

My pussy grows slick, and this time, I won't let rage consume me. This time, I will draw out their deaths, and draw out the pleasure that will ultimately get me ready for my henchmen.

I let out a squeal of excitement and start slashing. Painting myself in the blood of sinners.

Chapter 11

Somewhere between torturing the demons together, to finishing them off, to chopping them in pieces—I decided I no longer want to kill Zade.

That's never happened before, but deep down, I felt relieved. I had decided to kill Zade because I knew he was dangerous. But he didn't smell like rot—not like the true demons do. The hint of burnt roses told me that while he's dangerous, he's not dangerous towards the innocent.

Just like me. I'm not sure why it took me so long to realize that I was going to kill someone who has the same mission as me. I would've never forgiven myself.

Zade was nice enough to help me clean up the mess. He insisted on taking care of the bodies, so all I had to do was help him carry the numerous body parts to his car.

I sit on the hood of his Mustang, staring at the lifeless buildings and rides scattered across the open field. It's fascinating to see how haunting and desolate the fair looks when the occupants leave, and the lights extinguish. The same buildings and rides that are lit up with an array of colors now look as if they've been sitting on the muddy earth for centuries, devoid of life.

"How old are you, kid?" Zade asks from behind me. I turn to see him coming around the hood, having put the last of the human remains in his car. He said he didn't trust me to get rid of the bodies properly. And when I told him my henchmen would take care of it, he said the only henchman he trusts is himself.

It made me giddy. As if he was including himself in my little family. But sadly, he's given no indication he plans on ever seeing me again.

I shrug my shoulders, swinging my legs back and forth. I shiver as a cold breeze picks up, blowing tendrils of brown locks across my face.

"I don't know," I answer quietly, swiping the hair from my face and tucking it behind my ear. "I'm sure that I'm in my twenties."

He cocks a brow. Despite my best efforts, I shiver. I've never seen anyone cock their brow quite like he does. "How do you not know?"

I giggle, amused by that question. "How would I, silly?"

His raised brow plunges low. One end of his face to the other. I giggle again.

"Do you... not celebrate a birthday?"

I cant my head to the side, confused. "Why would I do that?"

He sighs and leans against the shiny black metal beside me. "The date you were born. What date was that?"

I shrug my shoulders again. "I have no idea. Daddy and Mommy never told me," I say. I've heard of birthday celebrations in my time outside of the cult. I made it a point to learn a lot of things, mostly by reading newspapers. Birthday celebrations are something I still don't quite grasp the point of.

"I grew up in a cult," I state tightly. "I wasn't born in a hospital, I was born in my parent's home. They never told me when that was."

He swallows. "No celebrations?"

This time, my laugh comes out bitter. "Daddy was the only one allowed to partake in any type of celebration, and it certainly wasn't because I was born."

The second the words leave my mouth, I realize how sad that sounds.

"I know that normal people usually know the dates they were born, but I was never taught to celebrate a birthday, so I never thought to ask when it was," I explain quietly.

"Normal people... yeah." He says that as if he's not included in that category. "Every year, they celebrate another year on this hellhole of a planet, as if it's something to be happy about," he muses quietly, his voice deepening.

Sounds like he's never celebrated a birthday either.

"You're not normal?" I ask, my curiosity piquing.

"The interesting people never are, demon slayer."

He straightens and walks around to his driver's side door. When he opens it, I take that as my cue to leave.

"Will I see you again?"

The question makes me feel vulnerable. I'm not even sure why I asked when it's my last day in Seattle. It's well past midnight and my time in this city is coming to an end soon. But we will be back next year. Maybe he'll remember me and come visit.

He stares at me hard, his face blank and unreadable.

"I think so, kid." He gets in his car and slams the door shut without another word. The car rumbles to life, the vibrations skittering up my spine. I hop off the car, trying to decide if I want to watch him drive away or not.

I feel an attachment to Zade now. I don't want to let him go, but I know I have to.

I've never killed with anyone else besides my henchmen before. It's indescribable, but I feel a bond with Zade now. I don't let go of bonds very easily. Even though he smells of fire and brimstone, he called me a friend. Most importantly, he helped me kill demons. And from the sounds of it, he plans on saving those girls too.

Maybe people with dark souls aren't all bad. Just because they're dark, that doesn't mean they're not redeemable. That doesn't mean there isn't good in there.

I groan. Now I'm going to question myself every time I cast my judgements!

With a smile on my face, I begin to walk towards my dollhouse, letting Zade go as I do. Despite how much I'd like him to be, he's not a henchman. He's a loner, and I get the feeling he likes it that way.

Besides, my henchmen love to play with me, and I don't think Zade has any interest in me that way. Based off the way he arrived at my dollhouse tonight, I think it's safe to assume he already has a special someone.

That's okay. I still had fun.

I've only made it a few steps when bright lights blind my vision. I raise a hand, confused by the sudden bright lights.

"Stop where you are!" A shout rings out from behind the glare. I can't see who is shouting at me, but they sound incredibly angry.

I pause, lift my chin to the air and sniff.

There's a mix of dirtiness and cleanliness in the air.

"Sibby! Get in the car!" Zade shouts from behind me. He's hanging halfway out of his car, eyes cast low in anger.

I glance back towards the lights, and this time I'm able to make out three cop cars parked haphazardly in the field. A total of five police officers are standing behind their respective doors, guns raised and aimed right at me and Zade.

Sadness and anger consume me all at once. My anger is shooting off in so many directions, I'm not exactly sure who to aim it at.

Zade? Or the demons we killed? Which of them alerted the police?

Plenty of anger is directed towards the police officers. They're trying to ruin my mission! The entire reason I was put on this planet, and police officers think they have a right to intervene.

"Sibby," Zade growls. "Now."

I sigh and turn back towards Zade.

"I can't leave my henchmen," I say sadly, offering a small smile.

"Sibby, they are—"

"I said freeze!" A police officer cuts in.

I snarl, whipping my head towards the officer.

"Go away! I work here."

The police officer shouts something back, but it becomes background noise when I see Mortis and Jackal peeking through the windows. I *won't* leave my henchmen. They've done *everything* for me. And I will do anything for them.

"Sibby," Zade starts again. "Please get in the car. They will arrest you if you don't."

I stomp my foot, feeling like I'm getting whiplash with all the orders being shouted at me from different directions.

"Zade, I'm not leaving them! Go, while you still can. I promise me and my henchmen will be okay."

He roughly wipes a hand down his face, muttering a guttural, "Fuck."

I see the decision the moment he makes it. He's going to leave me. Just like I'd asked. There's a twinge of sadness with that realization, but I don't let it settle. Zade and I may have extinguished evil together today, but we owe each other nothing.

And I think we've established an unspoken agreement that we won't rat each other out.

"Be safe, demon slayer."

Zade slams the door and the car lurches forward. Tires kick up mounds of dirt as he takes off at a breakneck speed.

"Fuck!" one of the officers shout. Two officers scramble back in one of the cruisers, slamming the doors shut a moment before the car speeds off after Zade, tires spinning and sending more mud flying.

I laugh loudly.

They'll never catch him. I know that in my bones.

Noticing the last three cops are distracted by the car chase, I take off towards the house.

"Hey! Stop right there or I'll shoot!"

I ignore him, already knowing they won't shoot. Not when they think they still have a chance of catching me.

"Hide, henchmen!" I scream as soon as I barrel through the door. Immediately, I see my men scrambling deeper in the house. I quickly crawl through one of my hidden doors, shutting the door quietly behind me just as the remaining three officers come stomping through the door.

That was close.

Quietly, I slinker through the hallways, and towards the staircase. There, I find my men waiting for me.

Mortis rushes towards me with wide eyes.

"What the fuck is going on, Sibby?" he whisper-shouts. His red eyes look terrifying in the low light.

"I don't know! They just showed up," I answer, my eyes wide with innocence. I knew my men weren't happy about being excluded from this execution, and this only cements their anger. I've never excluded them from a kill *ever*, but I just knew that Zade wouldn't have wanted them in the room.

And technically, he was after those demons first. If it wasn't for my intrusion, he would've taken care of them himself. Easily.

And neither of us would've gotten caught. Though I'm still baffled how that even happened.

Deep down, I know it wasn't Zade. He wouldn't have chopped four bodies into pieces, just to tell on himself and be chased with a car full of those body parts. Which means either one of those men managed to get some type of distress signal out to someone, or Mark's wife tattled. I'm not sure if I'll ever know.

"Where is she?" I hear one of the officers ask, urgency and confusion in his muffled voice.

The strobe lights and mechanical mannequins are still on in the rest of the house. Every few seconds, I'll hear expletives burst from their mouths or sharp yelps. I giggle every time, despite the gravity of this situation.

I'm going to have to leave Satan's Affair for good.

It doesn't matter if I kill them. There are officers that now know my face and know that I work in Satan's Affair. If they don't shut this place down for good, they sure as hell are going to be taking precautions from now on to make sure a little dolly isn't sneaking around inside the walls.

Eventually, they could start connecting missing person's to Satan's Affair, which will ultimately lead to me. A girl who has been murdering evil people for the last five years, leaving a deadly trail of mutilated bodies in unmarked graves.

My time here is over, and I want to rage and scream.

I *don't* like change.

Baine, Jackal, Cronus and Timothy gather in closer. Restless unease fills the air. They want to kill them—I can feel it. But two of the three cops are innocent. I don't kill innocent people, and they know that.

"What's the point in killing them when we're caught anyway?" I ask quietly, meeting each of their colored eyes.

"It will make me feel better," Mortis replies dryly, an evil smirk tipping his lips. With his devil makeup, he truly looks terrifying. I can't help but clench my thighs at the sight, my pussy pulsing steadily. I didn't get to come earlier when I was killing the demons. It didn't feel right to subject Zade to that, knowing he wouldn't appreciate it.

"It will waste time," Baine says quietly. "The two cops that drove off after that... *man* have already seen your face." He spits out the word like Zade personally wronged him. I supposed in a way, he did. "More could be on their way here now."

I nod my head, having already come to the same conclusion.

"How are we going to get away?" I ask. Our situation is beginning to settle heavily on my shoulders. I never thought I'd have to *leave.*

Jackal looks to the side, as if he's staring through the walls. "They have two cop cars out there, and it's safe to say the engines are still running. We can split up and each take one. That way they can't follow us."

My eyes widen. "We can't split up," I protest vehemently. The possibility of us getting separated sends a dose of panic into my bloodstream. Something could happen to one of our cars and the other would never know. "No. No splitting up. Let's just... slash the tires or something."

Jackal grabs my hand, noting the rising panic on my face. "Okay, okay. We stick together," he placates, his yellow eyes softening.

"I'll distract them, cause a commotion, while the rest of you escape. One of you slash the tires," Mortis directs.

We nod our agreement, the panic in my veins bleached out and replaced with adrenaline. I don't know if I've ever been in a car before. After I escaped from Daddy's,

I could only walk. I didn't have money for public transportation, and I refused to get in a car with a stranger.

It was by sheer luck that Satan's Affair happened to be in town when I got out of the compound.

My hand snaps out, and I grab onto Mortis's arm before he can walk away. I pull his arm until the length of his body is pressed into mine. He wraps his other hand around the back of my neck and brings me close, until his forehead rests against mine.

"I love you," I whisper, sliding my lips across his. He presses his mouth tightly against mine.

"I love you, too, baby girl. Be safe and kill them if you need to," he says before stepping away and rushing off into the maze of hallways.

My lip trembles. My henchmen and I had something good going, and I screwed it all up.

"Let's go, baby," Jackal says quietly, ushering me off. We all crowd around the small door right at the foyer. None of the officers are within sight, but there's no telling where exactly any of them are at the moment.

A loud crash sounds from above us, followed by a sharp yell.

"Hey! Get back here!"

I let my henchmen out first, the four of them squeezing through the door one at a time. It takes too long for them to file out, but finally I'm coming up behind them and rushing out the main door.

The brittle wind whips me in the face as I race off towards the still-running cop cars. I slip my pretty knife from the strap around my thigh and plunge it into one of the tires. Only for the knife to bounce back. These tires are way thicker than I gave them credit for. I grit my teeth and stab the knife in with all my strength, huffing in victory when it cuts through. I grind my knife against the tread, sweat breaking out across my forehead. A loud whistle pierces my ears as air escapes from the deflating tire.

"Hey!" A shout rings out from behind me. I quickly round the now useless car and head towards the other cruiser. The passenger door is already open and waiting for me, courtesy of Baine, who's behind the wheel. I dive into the seat and barely shut the door before the car is lurching forward, fishtailing as we take off.

"GET BACK HERE!"

I'm panting hard, my chest heaving as I'm blasted with excitement and a thrill so sharp, I can't help but let out a squeal of laughter. The car wavers as we tear through the field and onto the main road.

Urgent voices filter in from the radio on the dashboard. Panicked reports of a cop car being stolen and the other sabotaged, along with police jargon I don't understand. I do hear them say we've gone eastbound and that we're dangerous.

I giggle at the last part.

The rest of my men are piled into the backseat, cramped and uncomfortable, but with delighted smirks on their painted faces.

"You ever been in a car, baby?" Jackal asks from the back, amusement in his tone.

"No," I breathe, a wobbly smile on my face. Based off the speedometer, we're going almost 100mph. It's both exciting and nerve wracking.

The car swerves again, causing me to look over at Baine.

"Have you ever driven a car before?" I question.

I would have assumed so. I never got the opportunity to learn how to drive, but I would've thought my men had.

"Yes, but I've never been in a fucking car chase before so excuse me if I'm a little nervous."

I open my mouth to snap back but realize fighting with him will only worsen his driving. So, I close my mouth and let him focus.

The blare of sirens that reverberates from behind us has us all tensing in our seats. Several more sirens follow suit, until it sounds like a stampede of angry cop cars.

"Shit, fucking shit," Baine curses under his breath.

Blue and red lights flash in the review mirror, drawing closer by the second. Baine stomps on the gas hard, the car dangerously swerving side to side.

"Baine!" I shout. "Keep the fucking car straight!"

"I'm fucking trying!" Sweat pours down his face, his bone white knuckles tightening his grip on the wheel until they turn red.

The cop cars draw closer. I whip around in the seat, growling when my vision is obscured by the barrier and Cronus's fat head.

"Cronus, bend your head down!"

The car jerks and I'm forced to turn around and watch the car nearly careen off the side of the road and into a ditch.

Just barely is Baine able to right the car.

"How many cars are behind us?" I shout, no longer trusting to take my eyes off the road.

I stick my face into the review mirror, counting the cars just as Mortis announces, "Six."

Six?!

"Fuck," Baine mutters, leaning his body further in towards the wheel in concentration.

It takes all of two minutes before the cops are right on our tail. They're forced to keep a straight line as other cars are passing by on the other side of the road.

The car jerks again, and I just know it.

We're going to crash.

Baine's nerves are causing him to lose control of the car.

We careen to the left. Baine overcompensates and spins the wheel to the right, attempting to get us back on track. But he fails. The car jerks too quickly, and the car lifts up on one side. We turn completely sideways, the car losing control and bucking wildly as Baine keeps attempting to turn the wheel.

"Baine!" I screech just as the car is jerked violently. The sound of metal crunching follows a second later.

One of them hit us!

My head snaps to the side, hitting hard against the window right before the car is lifted. My entire body goes weightless, hitting against the roof of the car a second before my world spins tumultuously. It happens in slow motion, and too quickly all at once.

The car rolls four or five times, my body carelessly tossed around the car before we finally hit the ground in a violent jolt. My ears ring, a loud wailing reverberating in my skull.

It takes several moments before I realize the wailing is coming from my own mouth.

The car landed upright, but my body is twisted oddly in the seat, my head by the passenger side's floor. Baine's limbs are sprawled across mine, our bodies tangled in a mess of aching limbs. Groans of pain penetrate my ears, coming from Baine and in the backseat.

My men!

I try to sit up, but a piercing pain in my ribs forces me back down.

Oh my god, I hurt. I've never felt this type of pain in my entire life. Not even from Daddy's punishments.

My head pounds, blood dripping into my eyes.

"Baine?" I gasp, forcing myself up. My head spins and my vision darkens. The pain is literally blinding. I can't see or hear anything past it. I clutch my head in my bloodied hands, willing the pounding to cease so I can check on my men.

Before I can get ahold of myself, my body goes weightless again as I fall to the side. I was leaning heavily against the car door before it was jerked open. Hands grip my arms, firmly but not roughly. Shouting and voices filter through as I'm gently pulled out of the car.

Reality hits and I panic beneath their touches.

"Let me go!" I shout, wriggling against the hold. Blinding lights paint the world in reds and blues, but I can hardly get my vision to focus.

"Ma'am! Ma'am, please calm down!" a woman's voice shouts at me.

"My men! Where are my men?" I wail, continuing to wriggle. I can't see them, but I think I hear Mortis's voice and a panicked cry from Timothy.

Another pair of hands grab me, holding me still as I'm settled onto a stretcher. Its then I realize the woman is a paramedic.

"We're going to need to sedate her," the woman speaks above me, her voice getting lost in the turmoil inside my head. Binds are strapped across my chest and arms, holding me immobile. A brace is put around my neck, preventing me from turning my head.

They get the contraptions on me within seconds. Before I get a chance to look for my henchmen.

"Where are they?!" I scream, ignoring the blinding pain and continue to thrash as much as the binds will allow.

"She's going into shock," I hear another voice say. There's a small prick of a needle, there and gone before I can register what it was.

I continue to scream for my henchmen, but I can't move. I *need* to move!

"Everything is going to be okay, just calm down," the woman says. Dizziness consumes me, and then blackness bleeds into my sight. I try to blink away the impending darkness, but I can't fight it.

The last thing I hear is Mortis calling my name before I'm completely pulled under.

h.d. carlton

Epilogue

I slam my tray down on the table, scaring a few people around me and causing the slop on the tray to splatter on the white tables.

Fuck them. Fuck this food. Fuck this entire place.

"Sibel!" a guard yells from across the room. I don't even look at him. He has it out for me, I know he does. Ever since I've arrived in this god forsaken place, he's always watching me. The demon finds any reason to get me in trouble and send me back to my room.

I know the way he looks at me. He's scared of me.

He fucking should be.

"What!" I yell back. I sit down with a huff, already pissed off. The nurse came into my room at six o'clock in the morning to feed me more meds. I took them at first, when I first arrived here. But I stopped taking them a week ago.

I don't want to be drugged up anymore. The more comatose I feel, the more I start to forget my henchmen. They don't visit me in here. I haven't heard what happened to them after the car accident. How badly they were hurt, or if any of them even survived. The possibility of one of them being dead nearly *does* make me crazy.

No one will tell me. Maybe they were convicted of the murders, or maybe they also got sent to the loony bin.

Whatever the case, I miss them fiercely, and I don't ever want to forget them. They were—*are*—everything to me. If I lose any of them, I'll lose all my sanity and become the very thing everyone has always accused me of.

If they thought I was crazy before...

I would fucking belong in here then. In a lunchroom with *real* crazy people and they're all staring at me like *I'm* the one that's fucking cracked.

"Clean your act up, or you're going back to your room," he threatens, a stern look on his ugly fucking face. There's no way this man gets pussy. He's far too ugly, with his greasy cornflower blonde hair, pinched brown eyes and acne scars all over his cheeks. He's also too uptight, probably having been bullied his whole life so now he feels the need to take it out on anyone he deems inferior. Maybe I'll suck his dick later to loosen him up so he leaves me the hell alone.

I ignore him and angrily scoop up some applesauce onto my spoon and shove it in my mouth.

This day is only going to get worse. I have another appointment with Dr. Rosie today. She's a conniving bitch that's trying to convince me of false things. Over the past three months, she's been trying to convince me I'm crazy. Talk of severe *psychosis* and *delusions* have fallen from her and the nurses mouths a few times. Dr. Rosie diagnosed me with a bunch of bullshit I wasn't willing to listen to.

I'm not fucking *crazy*, I'm enlightened! I've been doing a goddamn service to this world by getting rid of the evil. Who else was going to do it? That's a question Dr. Rosie could never give me a straight answer to. She always spouts the same thing. *That's not for you to decide. You're not the judge and executioner.*

Yeah, whatever, bitch.

I am. I've been doing what everyone else is too weak to do. Sniffing and snuffing out the evil. And I'm being punished for it.

I'm busy glaring into my applesauce when I feel someone sit down next to me. I ignore whoever it is, too focused on my daydream of maiming every single employee in this place and escaping.

Every time I fantasize, I always see myself covered in blood and holding onto my pretty knife, running out of the building and straight into my henchmen's arms. They're all there waiting for me, big smiles on their made-up faces. They scoop me in their arms and tell me how proud they are of me.

And then they whisk me away and show me how much they missed me with their tongues and cocks.

The unwanted person leans too close to me. I get a whiff of poison berries, the kind Daddy had me pluck from the bushes and bake into pies when he deemed a follower unworthy.

I snap my head up, glaring at the intruder. Glenda. She's looking into my applesauce, a contemplative look on her face.

"Did the applesauce wrong you somehow?" she asks, the wrinkles on her face crinkling as she speaks.

She's an ancient woman. Apparently has been here since she was sixteen years old. There are rumors that she murdered her family with an axe because she believed they were all possessed by the devil. Chopped their heads off and then burned the bodies. I've never heard Glenda admit nor deny it. She doesn't speak about it at all.

For whatever reason, she's content in this place. It's safe for her, and it's all she's known for at least sixty years. I guess they've tried to release her several times, stating she's been rehabilitated and is no longer a danger to society. But every time, Glenda would attack a nurse, biting them until their flesh is ripped away. Just so she can stay in her home.

My brows furrow. "Why would you ask something so stupid?" I snap, before scooping another mouthful of applesauce into my mouth.

She didn't deserve that. I deflate.

"Sorry," I mutter.

Glenda has an odd smell to her. I've never smelt poison berries on anyone before, but I'm thinking she's like Zade—like *me*. Another one of those people who have blackness residing in their souls, but not completely consumed by it.

I wish someone else could sniff out evil the way I could, just so they would tell me what I smell like. Daddy would say I smell like a demon. That was his favorite thing to call me.

"You reek of sin and evil, Sibel. I don't know how I created such an abomination."

Glenda leans away, a smile on her face. "That's okay, child. We all have bad days."

"You say that as if good days exist," I murmur, my anger bleeding into sadness.

I'm really sad.

"They seem far away right now, but you'll see them again."

I don't answer. I don't believe a word coming out of her mouth. What does she know anyway? She's content spending the rest of her life in this hellhole. She's content being locked up, away from society because it's easier that way.

It's easier to give up on life. To have no will to live. To have no desire for freedom.

I want all those things and more.

I want my henchmen back. I want to go back to my life's mission. Executing the demons, all across the country. I want to feel my pretty knife plunging into flesh, tearing away at the sinewy muscles and hitting bone. To feel the warm blood spraying across my face and chest, coating my skin like oil. And then I want my henchmen to fuck me afterwards. Just like they always used to do.

Satan's Affair provided me a luxury unlike anything else, and I'll never have that again. They're the only travelling haunted fair that I know of, and just like I've suspected, they are now taking serious precautions to make sure another person doesn't slip under their radar.

"I'm never going to get out," I whisper, my heart breaking as I say it.

I spent a couple months in the hospital first, healing from a severe concussion, several broken bones, a punctured lung and nasty lacerations across my body. I was chained to the fucking hospital bed, scared and alone. I pleaded to see my henchmen, but they would just tell me to rest, refusing to let me see any of them.

They don't visit me here either, and after I asked Dr. Rosie if they could, she told me that we'd talk about it when I start healing. Always that stupid word. *Healing.* I *am* healed.

I was healed when I got to jail. And even more so when I saw the opportunity to kill another demon there.

My trial still isn't for quite a while, but they threw me in the mental institute after a month in jail. After that, they gave me a psych test and ultimately determined me as insane and delusional. What can I say? The demon smelt of rot and decay, and they looked so cute with a shank sticking out of their eye.

"Is that what your lawyer is saying?" Glenda asks, just as quietly.

I nod, a lone tear slipping down my pale cheek.

Another sad part—I don't have any make up in here to hide behind. In here, my face is bared to the world. It feels like walking into war without any armor. Without a sword and shield, and heavy metal to protect my body.

I just feel... vulnerable.

Every day, I look in the mirror—the kind that doesn't break, much to my dismay—and stare at the girl I've become. Pale face, round cheeks, plain brown eyes and a crooked nose. Dark circles rim my eyes, and my lips have become painfully chapped. My dark brown hair falls limply past my breasts, and every day, I'm tempted to cut it all off.

I stare at the mirror every day, and Mommy stares back at me.

"You look just like your mother. Are you even mine, Sibel?"

Every time he said that to me, I wanted to tell him I wasn't. Just for the small hope that he'd let me go. But then, I knew he'd kill Mommy for infidelity. None of the women there were allowed to bed anyone else but him.

I hate that I look like a ghost, which is why I was happy to cover it with makeup. I can't even bring myself to wear my pigtails anymore. Not when I don't have my doll face painted on and my pretty knife in my hand.

"I don't want to, but they say I'm crazy. I'm being forced to plead insanity. The lawyer said *Willowcreek Institute* will provide me the best possible life, compared to prison."

At least in prison, I could continue carrying out my mission. Prisons are filled to the brim with evil people. If I was sentenced to life, at least then I'd have nothing left to lose. I could keep killing, and still find some semblance of happiness. Even if my henchmen couldn't be by my side.

Glenda stays quiet for a moment.

"The outsiders—people that think they're normal—they don't understand people like us. We see the world for what it is. This Earth is layered, just like an onion, and we're only living in one of those layers. Us—*we* see the other layers. The energies that exist in this world and all the ugly and evil that comes alongside it. These layers are thin and strong entities can walk through the cracks, into other layers and wreak havoc."

"They say it's all in our head. But I think they're just suppressed. The things we see—they're not in our heads. They're in our faces. In our lives. And sometimes, in our bodies. They just can't see them."

I sigh. Despite what the doctors say, I'm *not* seeing or feeling anything that isn't actually there. Glenda's right. I know that the people I've killed were evil. I know that with every fiber of my being. I can smell their souls. I can smell the rot that's festering inside their bodies from the inside out. And I'm not wrong for extinguishing those rotted souls.

I'm not I'm not I'm not I'm not I'm not—

"Sibby?" My head snaps up. Glenda is staring at me, concern etched into her wrinkles. She's not looking at me like I'm crazy. Like the nurses or doctor would be. And especially the rotten guards that leer at us like we're scum. She's looking at me like she knows exactly what I'm feeling.

"Did you do it?" I whisper.

She stares back at me, an unreadable emotion flashing in her eyes.

"Did I do what, dear?"

"Did you kill your family? Because they were demons?"

She smiles—almost a tired smile.

"Honey, they weren't my family. They were Satan's."

That's all the confirmation I need.

Glenda's like me. She sensed the rot. She knew it to be true. And she got rid of them.

"I'm glad you're here, Glenda."

I don't say I'm glad *I'm* here because I'd rather be anywhere else but here. But I know Glenda is glad she's here, and since I'm forced to be here, I'm glad she is too.

She pats my hand.

"For what it's worth, I don't think what you did was wrong."

I open my mouth—to say what, I'm not sure. But I'm interrupted before I can figure it out.

"Sibel Dubois, let's go!" The same, greasy guard is yelling for me. Summoning me to see Dr. Rosie. I sigh, and Glenda winks and offers me a good luck.

Normally, I don't need good luck. But lately, I do. Dealing with Dr. Rosie is a headache, and she claims every session is a new breakthrough. If you ask me, the only thing she's breaking is my control to not fucking rip her eyes from their sockets.

The guard escorts me to her office, knocking once on the door.

Doctor Aberlyn Rosie is written on a pretentious gold plaque on the door. I want my pretty knife so I can carve the word *Bitch* into the plaque alongside her name. Only then, would I be able to stand to look at it.

"Come in, Sibby," she calls. A shudder works through me. She's *not* my friend. Only my friends call me that.

I shoot the guard a nasty glare, purely for just existing and it makes me feel better, before storming into the room. The first thing that greets my nose is a woodsy scent. Dr. Rosie smells like pine trees. I wrinkle my nose. I don't like the smell of pine trees, I like the smell of flowers.

"You're not allowed to call me Sibby," I gripe, aiming my glare her way. Her bleached blonde hair is pulled back in a low ponytail and pink lip gloss is painted on her lips today, making her sterile blue eyes pop.

Every day, she wears a different color lipstick. She says it brings a little bit of brightness to an otherwise depressing place. I wanted to pluck her pen from her breast pocket and shove it in her throat for saying that.

She says that like it's our fault it's depressing. No. It's *theirs*.

Crazy people are the most interesting people in the world if you'd just let them be who they are. Medicating and drugging people until they're mindless zombies would make *anyone* depressed, you dumb bitch.

"Still don't consider us friends?" she asks, her sculpted brow cocked with amusement. She doesn't look intimidating like Zade did. She just looks like she's trying to look cute and failing miserably.

What a miserable person.

"No," I snap. "Friends don't call other friends crazy."

"Sibby..." at my dark look, she clears her throat and corrects herself, her patient tone undeterred. "Sibel. I never said you were crazy. I said you're suffering from severe psychcosis and delusions. There are millions of people who have the same condition, and live normal lives."

Normal? What does normal even mean? Normal is subjective.

"I wouldn't say they live normal lives, Dr. Rosie. Seeing things *you* aren't capable of might be normal to them, but it certainly isn't the same definition you have declared as normal."

She smiles. "You're right, Sibel. I suppose it's very uncultivated of me to say their lives are normal." Before I can open my mouth and tell her about herself some more, she moves on. "Tell me about your henchmen."

My brow lowers and my heart sinks. Everything sinks.

"I don't want to talk about them," I growl.

She cocks her head. "Why is that, Sibby? Is it because they left?"

I sniff. Tears burn my eyes and line the edges of my lids. I refuse to let them fall. I refuse to show any kind of weakness in front of Dr. Rosie. She'll eat it up like a starved dog.

"Yes," I hiss through gritted teeth.

"Why do you think they left?"

I shrug a shoulder before crossing my arms and looking away. I'm sulking, and I have the right to. We promised we'd always be together, and they left me. They *lied*.

"Probably because they didn't want to get caught, too."

She writes something down in her notebook. The urge to stab the pen in her eye comes back with a vengeance. I'd really like to know what she writes about me.

Crazy. She's saying I'm fucking crazy.

"Sibby, how did you meet your henchmen?"

I sigh with impatience, but don't bother correcting her this time. "At Satan's Affair in a small town in Ohio. I had just escaped from Daddy's cult when I came across the travelling fair, and snuck into a haunted house after it closed down. I didn't have anywhere to sleep, nowhere warm, so I decided to sleep in one of the haunted houses for a night. There, I met my henchmen, standing over a dead body. They told me he was evil and it was like the world aligned. I knew my purpose in life but I knew it wasn't the right time to start until I was positive I could do it undetected. You know—by the *normal* people?

"My henchmen offered me that. They said I could stay within the walls and cast my judgements. Once I did, they'd help me carry out their punishment."

I had already told her all about Daddy's cult and how I ultimately escaped. It was five years ago when I had enough. He had just murdered an innocent woman for not following his rules. I don't even remember what exactly she did wrong anymore—Daddy always had rules that contradicted each other.

A woman cannot take a man's seed into her body unwed.

If you don't drink God's nectar, you will be damned to Hell for all eternity.

Don't fuck without being married, but oh no, if you don't suck on my cock, *you're* the unholy one.

I snapped when I saw an innocent woman dead because of a deranged man. If anyone was crazy—it was Daddy. He wasn't listening to God's voice in his head. He was listening to Satan's.

So I killed him. I grabbed the same knife that he stabbed into that woman's ear and turned it on him. I stabbed him well over a hundred times, until I was sitting on two hundred pounds of meat and bone, and I couldn't physically lift my arm anymore.

And then I set everyone free. Most were angry and cried. But I saw it deep in their eyes—they were relieved, too. They were just angry that they had to find their own purpose in life instead of blindly following the purpose that was handed to them by the devil.

"The other employees that worked in the dollhouse. Did any of them have friendships with your henchmen?" Dr. Rosie asks, bringing me back to the conversation.

I shrug. "Not that I know of. They stayed to themselves. They did their jobs and then helped me with mine."

Out of anger, I told my lawyer that I had help from my henchmen. My lawyer said they would look into it, but since then, he refused to talk to me about what's going on with them. If they've ever been caught. Or if there's an active manhunt for five deadly men.

He says I need to focus on myself right now, and he'll worry about the rest.

There's no point in trying to protect them now. They didn't protect me, and law enforcement already knew I had help since they were chasing after them, too.

"What about you? Did any of them know about you?"

I scoff. "No, I stayed inside the walls. The less they knew about me, the better. If no one ever saw me, then they wouldn't be able to pin anything on them in case I was caught."

Dr. Rosie hums, writing more baseless words down in her leather notebook. I wonder, is she one of those girls who write their feelings in journals? Does she take a pen to paper every time she's called a bitch by a patient? Does she talk about how unappreciated she is in her job, but if she could help just *one* person, it would all be worth it? I scoff again.

"Sibel, did you ever see your henchmen interact with other staff?"

I frown, furrowing my brow. "Why—"

"Just think about it. Humor me."

Irritation flares but I do it anyway. I think back to all the times during operation hours. I'd see staff look at them, but they always passed on by without talking to them. Everyone always seemed to look through them. Like they were so insignificant. My henchmen never seemed to notice or care.

"I guess not," I finally answer, confused on where she's going with this. So what if others didn't talk to them? Maybe they were scared of them.

"Why do you think that is?"

I open my mouth, but no sound comes out. "What kind of question is that?" I snap, my irritation growing. But it's not just irritation I'm feeling. It's fear, too.

My heart kicks into overdrive and Dr. Rosie eyes me.

"Do you think they're real?"

I jerk back with widened eyes, taken aback by her question but yet, not surprised by it. That question is exactly what I was fearing.

"Why the hell would you ask me that?"

Dr. Rosie shifts, as if she's settling in for a long conversation.

"Sibel. We found your henchmen."

Whiplash. She's jerking me back and forth. I can't keep up.

"Okay, and?" I snap. "Have they been apprehended?"

Her lips tighten into a thin line. "Sibel," she starts again. "They're mannequins."

My world tilts on its axis. A rock forms in my throat, steadily growing until I feel the need to claw at my throat. I can't breathe past it. My hands dart to the armrests, gripping them so tightly, my nails start to crack. Everything is spinning and Dr. Rosie's clinical voice is muffled, sounding like I'm trapped underwater and she's yelling at me from above.

"Sibby? Are you with me?" Her voice comes raging back, loud and abrasive.

I flinch away, but finally suck in a breath. "That's not true," I whisper. My chest is tight, and my eyes can't focus. "That's not true!" I say again, shouting the words.

Dr. Rosie rises from her seat and gently prods me to bend over. I listen and tuck my head between my knees and just try to breathe. I need to claw at my chest, my throat. Tear at the muscle until it lets me breathe again. Dr. Rosie holds my hand, reminding me that I *can* breathe.

Over the next several minutes, I'm completely seized by the panic gripping onto me like a leech. Until finally, I feel my chest loosening and my breathing evening out.

This isn't the first time I've found myself in this position in Dr. Rosie's office. It's why I hate coming here.

"You're wrong," I gasp, my breath still erratic and choppy.

Dr. Rosie sighs and makes her way back to her chair. "Sibel, you've had enough today. Let's continue this next week."

"No!" I roar, my spine snapping straight. It makes me dizzy but I power through until my doctor's blank face comes back into focus. "Tell me what you mean. Now."

She stares at me, seeming to contemplate if she should continue. She sighs again, but humors me. "All of the men that match the description of your henchmen—they're mannequins. They are mechanical mannequins that move, but they're not... living."

I shake my head, the tears I tried so hard to hold in are now streaming down my cheeks. She's lying. She *has* to be. I've seen them with my own two eyes. Touched them. Kissed them. Talked to them. For five years! Zade... he saw them, didn't he?

"But we... we were *together*," I insist, wiping snot from my nose. "I *felt* them."

Dr. Rosie keeps her face neutral, but something like sympathy shines in her blue eyes. I still want to stab them. Now more than ever.

"There were traces of your DNA found on the mannequins, Sibby. Along with sex toys."

I rear back once again. "I have never used those in my life!" I exclaim, aghast by her implications. I feel the blood rushing to my cheeks, and I'm angry that she's seeing me embarrassed. I've never been embarrassed in my life.

"You think people wouldn't have noticed me carrying around mannequins and fucking them?" I snap, disgusted by her implications.

She sighs. "You have a very complex condition. It's impossible to say exactly what your actions looked like, but it's safe to say that the majority of your interactions with your henchmen were hallucinated. I suspect after fair hours, when you wanted to feel a bit more of a connection is when you physically interacted with the mannequins.

"Otherwise, there's no evidence of you carrying them around. They weren't found in the cop car you stole, nor did any of the staff ever see the mannequins go missing during operating hours."

I shake my head. The memories, they are so real. So vivid. There's no way I imagined it. Flashbacks of all the ways they touched me. We laughed, cried and killed together. And she's telling me those memories are all fake. She's telling me I fabricated every single interaction. That's just not fucking possible.

"You were experiencing auditory, visual and somatic hallucinations," she continues, her tone clinical. "You were seeing, hearing and feeling things that weren't actually there. You saw the mannequins and brought them to life in your head. You were alone, scared and very lost, Sibby." I don't correct her this time. What she's describing is what I'm feeling right now. "So to bring yourself comfort in a time of loneliness, you created friends in your head, inspired by the mannequins in the house. They were just figments of your imagination."

I blink at her, shocked by her stupidity.

"Then who buried the bodies? Who cleaned up the messes? My henchmen always did that."

"*You* did, Sibel. Your henchmen were just an extension of *you.* Everything your henchmen did, was actually you. You completely disassociated from the acts you were doing because you were convinced it was your henchmen that was doing them."

Flashes of meaningless things flicker in my mind. A shovel gripped in my hand, cutting through dirt and grass. Blisters lining the palms of my hands. Sweat pouring down my face and neck as I throw bags of human remains in holes.

More flashes. Knocking over a mannequin so the cops would get distracted, and then running down the stairs. Getting into the car—the driver's wheel gripped in my hands. The foreign feeling of controlling a car...

Just small, sporadic glimpses that don't make any sense. None at all. Those were my henchmen doing those things... She's just trying to confuse me. She *has* to be. Trying to make me feel crazy so they can keep me locked in this hellhole forever.

I wipe more tears off my cheeks angrily, glaring at her through blurred vision.

"What else was fake then, huh? Were the people I killed fake, too? Are you saying they weren't demons?"

Dr. Rosie shakes her head slowly. "They were very real people, Sibby. They were human. The smells you associate with people is called olfactory hallucinations, and the belief that they were demonic were delusions. I suspect the trauma from your father and his cult is what triggered this. Due to the extent of abuse he inflicted on you, we suspect that he caused severe damage to your brain. He was an extremely sick man, Sibby, and he subjected you to awful abuse. Your brain was protecting itself in the only way it knew how.

"By the time you killed your father, he had brainwashed you with his own delusions. With the combination of brain damage and his brainwashing, that ultimately led you to create your own delusions and hallucinations. That these people were demons and you believed that you could smell the evil on them, or the purity on the others. This was how you justified killing.

"And your father *was* evil, Sibby. So, when you killed him, you felt you were doing something right. You felt it was your purpose to continue that path."

I shake my head, and keep shaking it, adamant she has everything wrong. The only thing she's right about is Daddy causing severe head trauma. One night, he had beat me so brutally, I was bedridden for months, and he had to pay a doctor to come see me on a daily basis. He had a niche for kicking me in the head, so Daddy causing some type of damage isn't surprising.

But she *is* wrong about the rest. I know this just as I know that my henchmen are real.

"So, you're trying to tell me the people I killed weren't evil?"

The detectives started combing through missing persons in all the locations Satan's Affair resides in for the past five years. They've been able to find numerous bodies and connect them to me, but they haven't found all of them yet. Some of them were too decomposed, and others were far too destroyed by my hands to get much DNA.

But they know I did it. They know it was me who killed them all.

"Some of the people they were able to identify did have records. But a lot of them were petty crimes. There's no way for us to really know if they were evil like you claimed."

I keep shaking my head. "My henchmen are real," I say, quite pathetically. "And those people were evil. I *know* it. Jennifer's boyfriend raped her! I heard it from her mouth, and he confessed before he died!"

Dr. Rosie nods her head slowly. "Jennifer Whitley?"

When I nod in confirmation, she writes something down her pad. "I don't know if that's true or not, but regardless, it doesn't matter, Sibby. Even if every single one of them were evil people, that wasn't for you to act on. You know that right?"

Her words prick at me, but instead of reacting in anger, I take a deep breath and dry my tears. Glenda's words come back to me. I may not be normal, but that doesn't mean I'm crazy. That doesn't mean what I'm seeing isn't real. Dr. Rosie—she can't see and smell the things I can. She wasn't blessed with gifts I was blessed with. I just have to remember that. No matter what she tells me, she's wrong. She's speaking from a place of ignorance.

How can you tell me I'm not seeing what I'm seeing, just because you can't see it, too? Why do the shortsighted people get to claim what is and isn't sane?

Slowly but surely, I calm.

"They're real," I say with conviction.

"We're real," a familiar voice whispers. My head snaps towards the voice, and I gasp when my eyes clash with familiar red eyes.

Mortis. Standing in the corner of the room, behind Dr. Rosie. Decked out in his red paint and red contact lenses. A small, knowing smile on his face.

"Do you see something, Sibby?" the doctor asks, her brow furrowing. My eyes slide back to her, and I work hard to keep my face blank.

"You're not allowed to call me Sibby," I reply.

"They tried to get rid of us," Mortis says, stepping away from the wall and walking up behind Dr. Rosie. Slowly, and methodically. She doesn't acknowledge him. Instead she's staring at me, a hard look on her face. "Did you stop taking the medications, Sibby?"

I nod, a small imperceptible dip of my chin as to keep the suspicions down from the doctor sitting across from me. Staring and dissecting. Trying to pick me apart and figure me out. She's just like the rest of them. She thinks I'm crazy.

Mortis stands directly behind her. The smirk on his face grows as he rests his red hands on her shoulders. Yet, she still doesn't acknowledge him. Doesn't even seem to feel him touching her. She just keeps staring at me.

"I know how to get us out of here, Sibby. You know what to do," he says, pointing towards the pen in her breast pocket. "Do it. Then we can be free, and then we can all be together again."

A slow smile spreads across my face.

Dr. Rosie scoots towards the end of her chair, now looking more alarmed. See? She can sense her death, just like I can sense the evil that surrounds us every day. "Sibby? What's going on?"

I stand. "Shh. It'll all be over soon, Dr. Rosie."

The End

Thank you for reading Satan's Affair!
I hope you found Sibby as fascinating as I did.

Want to learn more about Zade?
Continue reading to read the first chapter in the first book of his duet, Haunting
Adeline!

CHAPTER 1

THE MANIPULATOR

Sometimes I have very dark thoughts about my mother—thoughts no sane daughter should ever have.

Sometimes, I'm not always sane.

"Addie, you're being ridiculous," Mom says through the speaker on my phone. I glare at it in response, refusing to argue with her. When I have nothing to say, she sighs loudly. I wrinkle my nose. It blows my mind that this woman always called Nana dramatic yet can't see her own flair for the dramatics.

"Just because your grandparents gave you the house doesn't mean you have to actually *live in it.* It's old and would be doing everyone in that city a favor if it were torn down."

I thump my head against the headrest, rolling my eyes upward and trying to find patience weaved into the stained roof of my car.

How did I manage to get ketchup up there?

"And just because *you* don't like it, doesn't mean I can't live in it," I retort dryly.

My mother is a bitch. Plain and simple. She's always had a chip on her shoulder, and for the life of me, I can't figure out why.

"You'll be living an hour from us! That will be incredibly inconvenient for you to come visit us, won't it?"

Oh, how will I ever survive?

Pretty sure my gynecologist is an hour away, too, but I still make an effort to see her once a year. And those visits are far more painful.

"Nope," I reply, popping the P. I'm over this conversation. My patience only lasts an entire sixty seconds talking to my mother. After that, I'm running on fumes and have no desire to put in any more effort to keep the conversation moving along.

If it's not one thing, it's the other. She always manages to find something to complain about. This time, it's my choice to live in the house my grandparents gave to me. I grew up in Parsons Manor, running alongside the ghosts in the halls and baking cookies with Nana. I have fond memories here—memories I refuse to let go of just because Mom didn't get along with Nana.

I never understood the tension between them, but as I got older and started to comprehend Mom's snarkiness and underhanded insults for what they were, it made sense.

Nana always had a positive, sunny outlook on life, viewing the world through rose-colored glasses. She was always smiling and humming, while Mom is cursed with a perpetual scowl on her face and looking at life like her glasses got smashed when she was plunged out of Nana's vagina. I don't know why her personality never developed past that of a porcupine—she was never raised to be a prickly bitch.

Growing up, my mom and dad had a house only a mile away from Parsons Manor. She could barely tolerate me, so I spent most of my childhood in this house. It wasn't until I left for college that Mom moved out of town an hour away. When I quit college, I moved in with her until I got back on my feet and my writing career took off.

And when it did, I decided to travel around the country, never really settling in one place.

Nana died about a year ago, gifting me the house in her will, but my grief hindered me from moving into Parsons Manor. Until now.

Mom sighs again through the phone. "I just wish you had more ambition in life, instead of staying in the town you grew up in, sweetie. Do something more with your life than waste away in that house like your grandmother did. I don't want you to become worthless like her."

A snarl overtakes my face, fury tearing throughout my chest. "Hey, Mom?"

"Yes?"

"Fuck off."

I hang up the phone, angrily smashing my finger into the screen until I hear the telltale chime that the call has ended.

How dare she speak of her own mother that way when she was nothing but loved and cherished? Nana certainly didn't treat her the way she treats me, that's for damn sure.

I rip a page from Mom's book and let loose a melodramatic sigh, turning to look out my side window. Said house stands tall, the tip of the black roof spearing through the gloomy clouds and looming over the vastly wooded area as if to say *you shall fear me.* Peering over my shoulder, the dense thicket of trees are no more inviting—their shadows crawling from the overgrowth with outstretched claws.

I shiver, delighting in the ominous feeling radiating from this small portion of the cliff. It looks exactly as it did from my childhood, and it gives me no less of a thrill to peer into the infinite blackness.

Parsons Manor is stationed on a cliffside overlooking the Bay with a mile long driveway stretching through a heavily wooded area. The congregation of trees separates this house from the rest of the world, making you feel like you're well and truly alone.

Sometimes, it feels like you're on an entirely different planet, ostracized from civilization. The whole area has a menacing, sorrowful aura.

And I fucking love it.

The house has begun to decay, but it can be fixed up to look like new again with a bit of TLC. Hundreds of vines crawl up all sides of the structure, climbing towards the gargoyles stationed on the roof on either side of the manor. The black siding is fading to a gray and starting to peel away, and the black paint around the windows is chipping like cheap nail polish. I'll have to hire someone to give the large front porch a facelift since it's starting to sag on one side.

The lawn is long overdue for a haircut, the blades of grass nearly as tall as me, and the three acres of clearing bursting with weeds. I bet plenty of snakes have settled in nicely since it's last been mowed.

Nana used to offset the manor's dark shade with blooms of colorful flowers during the spring season. Hyacinths, primroses, violas, and rhododendron.

And in autumn, sunflowers would be crawling up the sides of the house, the bright yellows and oranges in the petals a beautiful contrast against the black siding.

I can plant a garden around the front of the house again when the season calls for it. This time, I'll plant strawberries, lettuce, and herbs as well.

I'm deep in my musings when my eyes snag on movement from above. Curtains flutter in the lone window at the very top of the house.

The attic.

Last time I checked, there's no central air up there. Nothing should be able to move those curtains, but yet I don't doubt what I saw.

Coupled with the looming storm in the background, Parsons Manor looks like a scene out of a horror film. I suck my bottom lip between my teeth, unable to stop the smile from forming on my face.

I love that.

I can't explain why, but I do.

Fuck what my mother says. I'm living here. I'm a successful writer and have the freedom to live anywhere. So, what if I decide to live in a place that means a lot to me? That doesn't make me a lowlife for staying in my hometown. I travel enough with book tours and conferences; settling down in a house won't change that. I know what the fuck I want, and I don't give a shit what anyone else thinks about it.

Especially mommy dearest.

The clouds yawn, and rain spills from their mouths. I grab my purse and step out of my car, inhaling the scent of fresh rain. It turns from a light sprinkle to a torrential downpour in a matter of seconds. I bolt up the front porch steps, flinging drops of water off my arms and shaking my body out like a wet dog.

I love storms—I just don't like to be in them. I'd prefer to cuddle up under the blankets with a mug of tea and a book while listening to the rain fall.

I slide the key into the lock and turn it. But it's stuck, refusing to give me even a millimeter. I jimmy the key, wrestling with it until the mechanism finally turns and I'm able to unlock the door.

Guess I'm gonna have to fix that soon, too.

A chilling draft welcomes me as I open the door. I shiver from the mixture of freezing rain still wet on my skin and the cold, stale air. The interior of the house is cast in shadows. Dim light shines through the windows, gradually fading as the sun disappears behind gray storm clouds.

I feel as if I should start my story with "it was a dark stormy night..."

I look up and smile when I see the black ribbed ceiling, made up of hundreds of thin, long pieces of wood. A grand chandelier is hanging over my head, golden steel warped in an intricate design with crystals dangling from the tips. It's always been Nana's most prized possession.

The black and white checkered floors lead directly to the black grand staircase—large enough to fit a piano through sideways—and flow off into the living room. My boots squeak against the tiles as I venture further inside.

This floor is primarily an open concept, making it feel like the monstrosity of the home could swallow you whole.

The living area is to the left of the staircase. I purse my lips and look around, nostalgia hitting me straight in the gut. Dust coats every surface, and the smell of mothballs is overpowering, but it looks exactly how I last saw it, right before Nana died last year.

A large black stone fireplace is in the center of the living room on the far left wall, with red velvet couches squared around it. An ornate wooden coffee table sits in the middle, an empty vase atop the dark wood. Nana used to fill it with lilies, but now it only collects dust and bug carcasses.

The walls are covered in black paisley wallpaper, offset by heavy golden curtains.

One of my favorite parts is the large bay window at the front of the house, providing a beautiful view of the forest beyond Parsons Manor. Placed right in front of it is a red velvet rocking chair with a matching stool. Nana used to sit there and watch the rain, and she said her mother would always do the same.

The checkered tiling extends into the kitchen with beautiful black stained cabinets and marble countertops. A massive island sits in the middle with black barstools lining one side. Grandpa and I used to sit there and watch Nana cook, enjoying her humming to herself as she whipped up delicious meals.

Shaking away the memories, I rush over to a tall lamp by the rocking chair and flick on the light. I release a sigh of relief when a buttery soft glow emits from the bulb. A few days ago, I had called to get the utilities turned on in my name, but you can never be too sure when dealing with an old house.

Then I walk over to the thermostat, the number causing another shiver to wrack my body.

Sixty-two goddamn degrees.

I press my thumb into the up arrow and don't stop until the temperature is set to seventy-four. I don't mind cooler temperatures, but I'd prefer it if my nipples didn't cut through all of my clothing.

I turn back around and face a home that's both old and new—a home that's housed my heart since I could remember, even if my body left for a little while.

And then I smile, basking in the gothic glory of Parsons Manor. It's how my great-grandparents decorated the house, and the taste has passed down through the generations. Nana used to say that she liked it best when she was the brightest thing in the room. Despite that, she still had old people's taste.

I mean, really, why do those white throw pillows have a border of lace around them and a weird, embroidered bouquet of flowers in the middle? That's not cute. That's ugly.

I sigh.

"Well, Nana, I came back. Just like you wanted," I whisper to the dead air.

"Are you ready?" my personal assistant asks from beside me. I glance over at Marietta, noting how she's absently holding out the mic to me, her attention ensnared on the people still filtering into the small building. This local bookstore wasn't built for a large number of people, but somehow, they're making it work anyway.

Hordes of people are piling into the cramped space, converging in a uniform line, and waiting for the signing to start. My eyes rove over the crowd, silently counting in my head. I lose count after thirty.

"Yep," I say. I grab the mic, and after catching everyone's attention, the murmurs fade to silence. Dozens of eyeballs bore into me, creating a flush all the way to my cheeks. It makes my skin crawl, but I love my readers, so I power through it.

"Before we start, I just wanted to take a quick second to thank you all for coming. I appreciate each and every one of you, and I'm incredibly excited to meet you all. Everyone ready?!" I ask, forcing excitement into my tone.

It's not that I'm *not* excited, I just tend to get incredibly awkward during book signings. I'm not a natural when it comes to social interactions. I'm the type to stare dead into your face with a frozen smile after being asked a question while my brain processes the fact that I didn't even hear the question. It's usually because my heart is thumping too loud in my ears.

I settle down in my chair and ready my sharpie. Marietta runs off to handle other matters, shooting me a quick *good luck*. She's witnessed my mishaps with readers and has the tendency to get secondhand embarrassment with me. Guess it's one of the downfalls of representing a social pariah.

Come back, Marietta. It's so much more fun when I'm not the only one getting embarrassed.

The first reader approaches me, my book *The Wanderer*, in her hands with a beaming smile on her freckled face.

"Oh my god, it's so awesome to meet you!" she exclaims, nearly shoving the book in my face. Totally a *me* move.

I smile wide and gently take the book.

"It's awesome to meet you, too," I return. "And hey, Team Freckles," I tack on, waving my forefinger between her face and mine. She gives a bit of an awkward laugh, her fingers drifting over her cheeks. "What's your name?" I rush out, before we get stuck on a weird conversation about skin conditions.

Geez, Addie, what if she hates her freckles? Dumbass.

"Megan," she replies, and then spells the name out for me. My hand trembles as I carefully write out her name and a quick appreciation note. My signature is sloppy, but that pretty much represents the entirety of my existence.

I hand the book back and thank her with a genuine smile.

As the next reader approaches, pressure settles on my face. Someone is staring at me. But that's a fucking stupid thought because *everyone* is staring at me.

I try to ignore it, and give the next reader a big ass smile, but the feeling only intensifies until it feels like bees are buzzing beneath the surface of my skin while a torch is being held to my flesh. It's... it's unlike anything I've felt before. The hairs on the back of my neck rise, and I feel the apples of my cheeks heating to a bright red.

Half of my attention is on the book I'm signing and the gushing reader, while the other half is on the crowd. My eyes subtly sweep the expanse of the bookstore, attempting to scope out the source of my discomfort without making it obvious.

My gaze hooks on a lone person standing in the very back. A man. The crowd shrouds the majority of his body, only bits of his face peeking through the gaps between people's heads. But what I do see has my hand stilling, mid-write.

His eyes. One so dark and bottomless, it feels like staring into a well. And the other, an ice blue so light, it's nearly white, reminding me of a husky's eyes. A scar slashes straight down through the discolored eye, as if it didn't already demand attention.

When a throat clears, I jump, snatching my eyes away and looking back to the book. My sharpie has been resting in the same spot, creating a big black ink dot.

"Sorry," I mutter, finishing off my signature. I reach over and snag a bookmark, sign that too, and tuck it in the book as an apology.

The reader beams at me, mistake already forgotten, and scurries off with her book. When I look back to find the man, he's gone.

"Addie, you need to get laid."

In response, I wrap my lips around my straw and slurp my blueberry martini as deeply as my mouth will allow. Daya, my best friend, eyes me, entirely unimpressed and impatient based on the quirk of her brow.

I think I need a bigger mouth. More alcohol would fit in it.

I don't say this out loud because I can bet my left ass cheek that her follow-up response would be to use it for a bigger dick instead.

When I continue sucking on the straw, she reaches over and rips the plastic from my lips. I've reached the bottom of the glass a solid fifteen seconds ago and have just been sucking air through the straw. It's the most action my mouth has gotten in a year now.

"Whoa, personal space," I mumble, setting the glass down. I avoid Daya's eyes, searching the restaurant for the waitress so I can order another martini. The faster I have the straw in my mouth again, the sooner I can avoid this conversation some more.

"Don't deflect, bitch. You suck at it."

Our eyes meet, a beat passes, and we both burst into laughter.

"I suck at getting laid, too, apparently," I say after our laughing calms.

Daya gives me a droll look. "You've had plenty of opportunities. You just don't take them. You're a hot twenty-six-year-old woman with freckles, a great pair of tits, and an ass to die for. The men are out here waiting."

I shrug, deflecting again. Daya isn't exactly wrong—at least about having options. I'm just not interested in any of them. They all bore me. All I get is *what are you wearing* and *wanna come over, winky face* at one o'clock in the morning. I'm wearing the same sweatpants I've been wearing the past week, there's a mysterious stain on my crotch, and no, I don't want to fucking come over.

She flips out an expectant hand. "Give me your phone."

My eyes widen. "Fuck, no."

"Adeline Reilly. Give me. Your. Fucking. Phone."

"Or what?" I taunt.

"Or I will throw myself across the table, embarrass the absolute shit out of you, and get my way anyways."

My eyes finally catch on our waitress and I flag her down. Desperately. She rushes over, probably thinking I found a hair in my food, when really my best friend just has one up her ass right now.

I procrastinate a little bit longer, asking the waitress what drink she prefers. I'd look through the drink menu a second time if it weren't rude to keep her waiting when she has other tables. So alas, I pick a strawberry martini in favor of the green apple, and the waitress rushes off again.

Sigh.

I hand the phone over, slapping it in Daya's *still* outstretched hand extra firm because I hate her. She smiles triumphantly and starts typing away, the mischievous glimmer in her eye growing brighter. Her thumbs go into turbo speed, causing the golden rings wrapped around them to nearly blur.

Her sage green eyes are illuminated with a type of evilness you would only find in Satan's Bible. If I did a little digging, I'm sure I'd find her picture somewhere in there, too. A bombshell with dark brown skin, pin-straight black hair, and a gold hoop in her nose.

She's probably an evil succubus or something.

"Who are you texting?" I groan, nearly stomping my feet like a child. I refrain, but come close to allowing a little of my social anxiety to air out and do something crazy like throwing a temper tantrum in the middle of the restaurant. It probably doesn't help that I'm on my third martini and feeling a tad adventurous right about now.

She glances up, locks my phone, and hands it back a few seconds later. Immediately, I unlock it again and start searching through my messages. I groan aloud once more when I see she sexted Greyson. Not texted. *Sexted.*

"Come over tonight and lick my pussy. I've been craving your huge cock," I read aloud dryly. That's not even all of it. The rest goes into how horny I am and touch myself every night to the thought of him.

I growl and give her the filthiest look I can manage. My face would make a dumpster look like Mr. Clean's house.

"I wouldn't even say that!" I complain. "That doesn't even sound like me, you bitch."

Daya cackles, the teeny little gap between her front teeth on full display.

I really do hate her.

My phone pings. Daya is nearly bouncing in her seat while I'm contemplating googling *1000 Ways to Die*'s contact information so I can send them a new story.

"Read it," she demands, her grabby hands already reaching for my phone so she can see what he said. I jerk it out of her reach and pull up the message.

GREYSON: About time u came to your senses, baby. Be over at 8.

"I don't know if I've ever told you this, but I really fucking hate you," I grumble, giving her another scowl.

She smiles and slurps on her drink. "I love you too, baby girl."

"Fuck, Addie, I've missed you," Greyson breathes into my neck, humping me against the wall. My tailbone is going to be bruised in the morning. I roll my eyes when he slurps at my neck again, groaning when he rolls his dick into the apex of my thighs.

Deciding I needed to get over myself and blow off some steam, I didn't cancel on Greyson like I wanted to. Like I *want* to. I regret that decision.

Currently, he has me pinned against the wall in my creepy hallway. Old fashioned sconces line the blood red walls, with dozens of family pictures from generations in between. I feel like they're watching me, scorn and disappointment in their eyes as they witness their descendant about to get railed right in front of them.

Only a few of the lights work, and they just serve to illuminate the spiderwebs they're crawling with. The rest of the hallway is shadowed entirely, and I'm just waiting for the demon from The Grudge to come crawling out so I have an excuse to run.

I would definitely trip Greyson on the way out at this point, and not one inch of me is ashamed.

He murmurs some more dirty things into my ear while I inspect the sconce hanging above our heads. Greyson said in passing once that he's scared of spiders. I wonder if I can discreetly reach up, pluck a spider from its web, and put it down the back of Greyson's shirt.

That would light a fire under his ass to get out of here, *and* he'd probably be too embarrassed to talk to me again. Win, win.

Just when I actually go to do it, he rears back, panting from all the solo French kissing he's been doing with my throat. It's like he was waiting for my neck to lick him back or something.

His copper hair is mussed from my hands, and his pale skin is stained with a blush. The curse of being a redhead, I suppose.

Greyson has everything else going for him in the looks department. He's hot as sin, has a beautiful body and a killer smile. Too bad he can't fuck and is a complete and utter douchebag.

"Let's take this to the bedroom. I need to be inside of you now."

Internally, I cringe. Externally... I cringe. I try to play it off by jerking my shirt over my head. He has the attention span of a beagle. And just like I suspected, he's already forgotten about my little blunder and is staring intensely at my tits.

Daya was right about that, too. I *do* have great tits.

He reaches up to tear the bra from my body—I probably would've smacked him if he actually ripped it—but he freezes when loud banging interrupts us from the main floor.

The sound is so sudden, so violently loud that I gasp, my heart pounding in my chest. Our eyes meet in stunned silence. Someone is pounding on my front door, and they don't sound too nice.

"Are you expecting someone?" he asks, his hand dropping to his side, seemingly frustrated by the interruption.

"No," I breathe. I quickly tug my shirt back on—backwards—and rush down the creaky steps. Taking a moment to check outside the window next to the door, I see the front porch is vacant. My brow furrows. Letting the curtain fall, I stand in front of the door, the stillness of the night closing in on the manor.

Greyson walks up beside me and looks over at me with a confused expression.

"Uh, you gonna answer that?" he asks dumbly, pointing at the door as if I didn't know it was right in front of me. I almost thank him for the directions just to be an ass, but refrain. Something about that knock has my instincts blaring Code Red. The knock sounded aggressive. Angry. Like someone had pounded on the door with all their strength.

A real man would offer to open the door for me after hearing such a violent sound. Especially when we're surrounded by a mile of thick woods and a hundred-foot drop into the water.

But instead, Greyson stares at me expectantly. And a little like I'm stupid. Huffing, I unlock the door and whip it open.

Again, no one is there. I step out onto the porch, the rotting floorboards groaning beneath my weight. Cold wind stirs my cinnamon hair, the strands tickling my face and sending shivers racing across my skin. Goosebumps rise as I tuck my hair behind my ears and walk over to one end of the porch. Leaning over the rail, I look down the side of the house. No one.

No one on the other side of the house, either.

There could easily be someone watching me in the woods, but I have no way of knowing with it being so dark. Not unless I go out there and search myself.

And as much as I love horror films, I have no interest in starring in one.

Greyson joins me on the porch, his own eyes scanning the trees.

There's someone watching me. I can feel it. I'm as sure of it as I am about the existence of gravity.

Chills run down my spine, accompanied by a burst of adrenaline. It's the same feeling I get when I watch a scary movie. It begins with the beat of my heart, then a heavy weight settles deep in my stomach, eventually sinking to my core. I shift, not entirely comfortable with the feeling right now.

Huffing, I rush back into the house and up the steps. Greyson trails behind me. I don't notice he's in the middle of undressing as he walks down the hallway until he steps into my room after me. When I turn, he's stark naked.

"Seriously?" I bite out. What a fucking idiot. Someone just banged on my door like the wood personally put a splinter in their ass, and he's immediately ready to pick up where he left off. Slurping on my neck like one would slurp jello out of a container.

"What?" he asks incredulously, splaying his arms out to his sides.

"Did you not just hear what I heard? Someone was banging on my door, and it was kind of scary. I'm not in the mood to have sex right now."

What happened to chivalry? I would think a normal man would ask if I'm okay. Feel out how I'm feeling. Maybe try to make sure I'm nice and relaxed before sticking their dick inside me.

You know, read the fucking room.

"You serious?" he questions, anger sparking in his brown eyes. They're a shitty color, just like his shitty personality and even shittier stroke game. The dude gives fish a run for their money, the way he flops when he fucks. Might as well lay out naked in the fish market—he'd have a better chance of finding someone to take him home. That person is not going to be me.

"Yes, I'm serious," I say with exasperation.

"Goddammit, Addie," he snaps, angrily swiping up a sock and putting it on. He looks like an idiot—completely naked save for a single sock because the rest of his clothes are still thrown haphazardly in my hallway.

He storms out of my room, snatching up articles of clothing as he goes. When he gets about halfway down the long hallway, he stops and turns to me.

"You're such a bitch, Addie. All you do is give me blue balls and I'm sick of it. I'm done with you and this creepy fucking house," he seethes, pointing a finger at me.

"And you're an asshole. Get the fuck out of my house, Greyson." His eyes widen with shock first, and then narrow into thin slits, brimming with fury. He turns, cocks his arm back and sends his fist flying into the drywall.

A gasp is ripped from my throat when half of his arm disappears, my mouth parting in both shock and disbelief.

"Since I'm not getting yours, thought I'd create my own hole to get into tonight. Fix that, bitch," he spits. Still sporting only one sock and an arm full of clothes, he storms off.

"You dick!" I rage, stomping towards the large hole in my wall he just created.

The front door slams a minute later from below.

I hope the mysterious person is still out there. Let the asshole get murdered wearing a single sock.

The Cat & Mouse Duet is now complete!
Order Haunting Adeline today or read for free on
Kindle Unlimited.

For My Readers

Whatever this book made you feel, I would be entirely grateful for you if you would consider leaving a review on Amazon or Goodreads. Author's livelihoods are centered around your feelings and thoughts, and I would absolutely love to hear them. Reviews and sharing your love mean the world to me, and they mean the world to author's as a whole.

Want sneak peaks, exclusive offers, and giveaways?

Join my Facebook group <u>H. D. Carlton's Warriors</u> or subscribe to my <u>newsletter</u>

More Books by the Author

Acknowledgments

First and foremost, as always, I thank *you*. My readers. I would be nothing without any of you, and I love and appreciate every single one of you. Thank you from the bottom of my heart for the love and support you bring me every day.

Secondly, thank you so much to my family for being the best support system I could ever ask for. I don't think I would be where I am today without any of you.

My alpha readers, May and Amanda, I love you both dearly. You two are my rocks. And thank you for being so supportive and loving.

My beta readers, you guys kick ass. Seriously. This book definitely wouldn't be what it is without any of you. Your eagle eyes helped make Satan's Affair perfect.

Sarah, you have become such an important person to me! Thank you times a million for editing my books and making them crispy clean. You are an amazing person to lean on and I'm forever thankful for you.

About The Author

H. D. Carlton is an International Bestselling Author. She lives in Ohio with her partner, two dogs, and cat. When she's not bathing in the tears of her readers, she's watching paranormal shows and wishing she was a mermaid. Her favorite characters are of the morally gray variety and believes that everyone should check their sanity at the door before diving into her stories.

Learn more about H. D. Carlton on hdcarlton.com. Join her newsletter to receive updates, teasers, giveaways, and special deals.